Out on a Limb

by

Allison Thorpe

A Family Tree Mystery, Book Two

Copyright Notice
This is a work of fiction. Names, characters, places, and incidents are either the product of the author's imagination or are used fictitiously, and any resemblance to actual persons living or dead, business establishments, events, or locales, is entirely coincidental.

Out on a Limb

COPYRIGHT © 2024 by Allison Thorpe

All rights reserved. No part of this book may be used or reproduced in any manner whatsoever without written permission of the author or The Wild Rose Press, Inc. except in the case of brief quotations embodied in critical articles or reviews.
Contact Information: info@thewildrosepress.com

Cover Art by *The Wild Rose Press, Inc.*

The Wild Rose Press, Inc.
PO Box 708
Adams Basin, NY 14410-0708
Visit us at www.thewildrosepress.com

Publishing History
First Edition, 2024
Trade Paperback ISBN 978-1-5092-5783-6
Digital ISBN 978-1-5092-5784-3

A Family Tree Mystery, Book Two
Published in the United States of America

Dedication

For Pam – Thank you for answering all my silly questions

And, always, for Taura

Chapter 1

The bald man in the bulky tweed coat had been following me for several blocks. Usually, I was pretty good at spotting the people looking to capitalize on last year's murder and Hill House fiasco. Most were reporters; some were tourists seeking leftover thrills; there were even a few oddballs wanting autographs. Too bad my old friend Rita had moved to New York. She always craved occasions to highlight drama.

I turned down Clark Hill Street and cut through Sherman Park hoping Will Pepper might be around. It would be nice to have the old veteran's set of eyes to check if someone was tailing me. Why had Poe chosen this week to go off to some training counsel on counterterrorism? The newly appointed Parkville Chief of Police Alan Poe, lifesaver and the man who had filled my daydreams for the past few months, would have known what to do in this instance.

It seemed like everyone connected with the Hill House murder last year had profited: Poe rose in rank, ex-neighbor and crime-solving buddy Rita Starr now graced the byline of a major big city newspaper, and even Albie my parrot got a bit of notoriety out of it all. I was the only one who shunned the spotlight.

Sherman Park was full of old soldiers taking advantage of the early spring weather, the daffodils, and the young girls playing soccer in the next field over. I lowered myself onto one of the benches and scanned the landscape. I couldn't spot the tweed-coated hulk anywhere. Was I just being paranoid? He didn't look like the typical adventure-monger or tourist. My brain twirled like a pinwheel in a tornado at the possibilities of who he could be.

I tried to relax. It felt peaceful to sit here. The sun lustered the sky like a hard-polished disc and declared winter woes were through having their way with us. Poe had promised Hawaii after Christmas, but his recent appointment meant more hours on the job and less time to play. Maybe once he settled in, we could escape somewhere. I closed my eyes and fantasized about jetting to Hawaii, strolling the welcoming white beaches, frolicking among the frisky blue waves. I tried to imagine what Poe would look like in something other than the suits he always wore, when the world suddenly went cold.

My eyes flew open to see the tweed-shrouded man standing in front of me, blocking the sun, his cumbersome coat hiding all manner of imagined evils.

"Ah, yes, I remember those questioning blue eyes." His deep voice echoed in the stillness.

I felt around in my backpack for the pepper spray I always carried.

"No need for that, Miss Turner." He motioned with a hand and a tilt of the head to ask if he could share the bench and then accepted my silence for acquiescence. I felt the bench give an almighty shift under his vastness. Now that he was close, the air reeked of chemicals and decay. He could have been the headliner at a mothball convention.

"How do you know my name?" Words finally

shambled their way out of my mouth.

He fingered a fat cigar and took his time lighting it before he turned to me. "Because, my dear, I'm your uncle."

****

It was startling news, but so many weirdoes had crawled out of the sewers this past year, I wasn't totally surprised. I threw out something a bit devious: "So you are my father's brother then?"

"Nice try, sweetie." He puffed out a stream of smoke, adding layers to his rank perfume. "We both know that man was a mystery, a myth, whatever your so-called mother put on your birth certificate."

"So-called?" I turned around on the bench to face him, trying hard not to choke on the waves of stench. His face hung in coarse folds, the eyes just pudgy dots, and the unruly eyebrows could have registered their own zip code. The sweat on his smooth head glittered like morning dew.

"She wasn't your real mother." His face exhibited a sadness as he continued to bully the sweet spring air with his smoke.

"And just how do you know that?" I was getting annoyed at his game.

"Because she was my sister, and she told me everything."

"I beg your pardon?" It wasn't what I expected.

"Elizabeth was my sister or rather Lizzie as she rebranded herself. Lizzie Taylor." He huffed the cigar for a bit before going on. "You can call me Uncle Mickey."

"My mother was your sister?" I realized my echo sounded a lot like Albie, my parrot.

"We got separated when we were young. Lizzie

went with our mother, and I went to live with dear old Dad. We connected later in life for, well, let's just say more profitable ventures."

I wavered between disbelief, wariness, and wanting to jump into the deep end and madly splash around. Sticking a toe in the water, I waded in, deciding on the middle ground. "Why should I believe you? My mother's dead. Anyone could come along and say that."

"I've got the documents to prove it. Now let me ask you something. Were you with your mother when she passed? Can you prove that?"

"Yes." It seemed like an odd question, but he turned sharply and searched for truth in my face.

"Did she mention me?" he asked. "At the end?" I saw the tenseness in his neck. Even the cigar seemed to still its fume.

"No." I wondered where this was leading.

He sighed. "I guess she never got around to talking about me." His shoulders slumped deeper into the coat, and he closed his eyes.

They stayed shut so long I thought he might have fallen asleep. I moved a bit on the bench, hoping I could slip away unnoticed, but his eyes popped open, and he muttered out the side of his mouth. "But if you have… information about her last job, I can help dispose of the merchandise for you. I'm staying at the Grady Hotel. Room 306. Come tonight at seven and I'll spill it all." He heaved his mothy mass off the bench and lumbered off without another word.

I did what any good researcher-turned-involuntary-sleuth would do: sat for a few minutes, took several deep breaths, and then followed him. My sleeves had grown a few tricks.

Me: El Turner, mild-mannered genealogist and stay-at-home researcher, had recently embarked on researching a family tree of utmost importance—mine. My move to Parkville had been to care for my dying mother. At her funeral, she sent me a message through her attorney: *I am not your mother.* It was all too much to process at that point, but my head was now in the right place to find out. So far, I had had no luck. If she wasn't my mother, who was? And why had she pretended to be? Had I been adopted? Kidnapped? Given away? Why had she felt the need to tell me? My head dizzied with the familiar scenarios that had haunted my brain waves over the past few months. This dropped-from-space uncle was almost too much of a coincidence.

I kept well behind him, shadowing trees and buildings, but he was true to his word. He ambled into the Grady Hotel. The building was famous. Or rather infamous. Renting rooms by the minute, hot poker games in the basement, police raids so often there was no thrill anymore in hearing about them. It was known as the Shady Grady, and Poe had it on his list of places to clean up. I turned around and left.

When I got back home, I ran the event through for Albie. The African gray parrot I inherited after my mother's death had become a feathered companion and sounding board for my erratic life.

"Oh, Albie!" I threw my jacket and backpack on a nearby chair and hurried over to his cage. "You won't believe this, but this old guy walks up and tells me he's my uncle. What do you think? Does it sound real or just like another crazy reporter? He didn't dress like a reporter though. What reason would he have for luring me to the Grady?" I laughed. "Okay, don't answer that!"

Talking aloud to the parrot often made sense of confusion. It was something that had slowly evolved after the parrot had been dumped on my doorstep. "Damn, Albie. I never even asked his name or for any identification. What is wrong with me? Some fact searcher I am!" I shook my head in disgust at the missed opportunity, the stupid oversight. I could hear Rita tsk-tsking all the way from New York. Her constant presence in my apartment had always been a rude interruption to my work, but now that she was gone, I sorely missed it. She was like the annoying little sister I never had and one I didn't know I wanted.

"Damn, Albie," the bird echoed. "Damn, Albie." Too late. Swearing around a talking bird was a lot like cursing in front of a toddler. It was bound to come back and bite one's ass when least expected.

"There was one odd thing. The man said my mother's name was Lizzie Taylor." I paced in front of the cage. "It's true that Elizabeth was her name, but she went by Lizzie Turner, not Taylor. It would certainly suit her more to be known as Elizabeth Taylor." We had been out of touch for well over a decade, so I had come to know the woman better only during her dying days. Even then, she still favored the tight sweaters, bleached wavy hair, and 1950s Hollywood movie smile. I gave Albie a treat and continued. "She certainly loved that era of Hollywood. After all, she named me Lana Turner."

"Lana. Lana." Albie's excited squawking filled the room. He sidestepped back and forth along his perch, head bobbing like some mechanical windup toy.

I wandered around the small apartment. What could he want from me? Did I dare go to his hotel room alone? Should I make a list of questions to ask him? Maybe I should leave word with Jenny Lane, my purple-haired, kombucha-sipping, tai chi-loving, older neighbor. She was aware of what I had endured the past year and watched over me like the classic motherly hen. I could tell her I was going out, but I certainly could not tell her where.

I stopped in front of the cage. "Yes, that's exactly what I'll do, Albie. I'll tell Jenny I have to be somewhere and if I am not home by nine to call the police. Or maybe I should wait for Poe to get back into town." I continued my pros and cons in front of the bird, but I already knew what I had decided. "But if I wait, this mystery man might leave, and I'll never find out the truth. Do I really want what he has to offer? Oh, why do these things happen to me?" I stomped my foot. My questions seemed to hang in the air like plump, tempting grapes I was afraid would turn sour once they hit my mouth. I took my own advice and made a list of things I really wanted to know. If he was related to my mother, he should have the answers.

I tried doing research for a client to pass the time, but my fingers didn't want to play with the keyboard. They were as twitchy as the rest of me. A squirrel on caffeine would appear calmer. Food held no appeal, and in the end, I sat and stared out the window, tapping my foot and contemplating several future outcomes, none of which were to my liking.

Finally, I brushed my boring brown hair, wound it back into the braid I had begun to wear, grabbed my coat, and slipped a note under Jenny's door just in case. I didn't think I was in the right state of mind to answer her questions, and I knew she would be able to spot the lies.

The days were getting longer, but the dim evening

was slowly advancing. The sky cast a faded pink ribbon across the horizon that I hoped was a good omen. I crept most of the way, checking my back as I went, unsure of what dwelled in the dimness. I had tried Poe's number before I left, but it continued to go to voicemail.

I wasn't biblical, but I felt the shivers of Daniel sneaking into the lion's den. The roaring pounded in my ears.

****

I shied away from the elevator and ducked around the corner to the stairs. No one was at the desk when I entered the Grady Hotel lobby. I saw a man whom I assumed to be the manager in a back office with his feet up watching TV. According to the gunshots and sirens, it sounded like an episode of some police action series. The warped wooden stairs creaked and groaned like a sad Halloween horror movie. When I opened the door into the third-floor corridor, I stopped and listened. I thought I heard raised voices, but they were muffled and could have been a radio. The walls in this place were not exactly insulated; rice paper had more starch than these walls. No one was around.

Suddenly a distraught woman flew around the corner, knocked into me, grabbed my arm to steady herself, and ran down the stairs. It happened so quickly, I didn't notice much except for dark hair under a baseball hat and large sunglasses covering a good part of her face. Sunglasses at night? So much craziness had been written about the Grady, I shouldn't have been surprised. Still, it was a warning to be cautious. I crept onward.

Room 306 was at the end of the long hallway. I knocked and put my ear to the door. I thought I heard scrabbling. I hoped there were no rats around. I reached around for my backpack before realizing I had left it at home. No pepper spray. It also meant no phone. I had spent so much time imagining what was to come, I had given no thought to preparing for what might happen. Did I have a brain left at all?

The second time I rapped, the door inched open a bit. This wasn't good.

"Hello? Hello Mr…" I felt like an idiot again not getting the man's last name. "Uncle Mickey?"

I pushed the door wider. Then I saw him. Or his rundown shoes anyway; they seemed right at home in this environment. Uncle Mickey appeared to be lying on the floor between the two beds. I worked my way slowly into the room and stopped. He sprawled spread eagle on his back, the heavy coat thrown over him. Was he sleeping? I feared the worst. He moved an arm, and I screamed.

"Diamond" came as a soft whisper.

"What?" I asked, leaning closer. There wasn't much space between the beds, and I didn't want to fall on top of him.

"Dixie," dribbled slowly out of his mouth.

"What? What did you say?"

I lifted a corner of his coat and saw the knife and the blood. Not another knife murder! Echoes of last year's killing rattled around in the still air. He gurgled one last breath, and his head lolled to the side. I heard the rustle of clothes behind me.

"Oh my god! She killed him! I saw her. She killed that man! Help! Help!" a woman hollered.

Before I could say anything, the doorway filled with people.

"Don't move, young lady," a deep voice shouted. It

was the manager with a baseball bat in his hand, seeming on the verge of violence, almost growling as he moved closer.

I put up my hands, sat on the edge of the bed away from the body, my back to the growing crowd, and waited for what I knew was coming.

****

Police were all over the room. It was clearly more excitement than they were used to in this place, and that was saying a lot. Two attendants fussed over the body, moving the bed nearest the door out of the way for their wheeled stretcher. No one thought to question me, so I stood and started inching slowly out of the picture. Maybe I could ease an escape in all the commotion.

"Not so fast!" A blue uniformed muscle man blocked my way. At first, I thought it might be Reb Wilson, Rita's boyfriend, before I remembered he had moved to New York to be near her.

"Just stretching my legs, officer. Do you mind if I get some air?"

"I think you better stay put." He looked me up and down.

"Yes, don't let her leave," cried the manager, a short, broad-shouldered brute with bad teeth. "That's the lady that stabbed him!" He pointed the baseball bat at me.

"I did no such thing!" I stared at him. "I just knocked at the door, it opened, and I saw him on the floor."

"Did you touch anything on the body?" the officer asked.

"No."

"Yes, she did," the nosy manager shouted. "Look at her coat. She has blood all over the sleeve."

I looked down and saw red streaks on my new tan jacket. "I have no idea where that came from," I retorted.

"Are you sure you didn't touch the body."

"Positive." I remembered the woman in the hallway. "Wait. There was a lady in the corridor as I came up the stairs. She was running and almost knocked me down. I remember she grabbed my sleeve."

"Oh sure. A likely story." The manager sneered. He was as annoying as a rabid mosquito.

"No. Really. She must have come out of this room. She could be the murderer! You must look outside. She may have already gotten away." I pointed toward the window.

"Likely story," manager repeated, moving a wad of tobacco around in his mouth and looking like he might spit on the floor.

"Sir." The officer gestured for the manager to go out into the hall. "Ma'am. Can you describe her?"

"Dark hair. Baseball cap. Sunglasses."

"Not much to go on." He took out a notebook. "What kind of clothes was she wearing?"

"It all happened so fast; I can't be sure. Maybe a dark jacket and blue jeans."

"Did you know the victim?" the officer asked.

"No. I think his first name was Mickey."

"What were you doing in his room?" The officer had more questions than I had answers. Everything I said sounded as sketchy as the manager's dental plan.

"He claimed to be my uncle and said he had information about my family."

The officer stopped writing, scrunched his eyebrows, and peered into my eyes. "He was your uncle, and you don't know who he was? That doesn't make sense."

"It's a long story, but I never met the man. He came up to me today in the park and said he was my uncle. He told me he had information about my mother and to come to this hotel tonight. He gave me the room number. That's all I know."

"Sit down over there until we're finished here. You're going to have to come down to the station to straighten all this out." He regarded me as either a lunatic or a suspect, a look dubious enough to have covered either.

I dropped back down onto the edge of the farthest bed, my back to the room and the dead body and looked out the window. Night smothered the glass, and the room's light mirrored a distorted reflection of the scene behind me. Police moving here and there, the manager still waving his bat around, curious onlookers poking their heads in for a thrill. A large figure moved in and dominated the doorway. He was dressed in a dark suit and somber tie looking more like he had come from a boardroom than the Shady Grady. I felt his eyes drill intently into my back. Gingerly, I turned around, but he had disappeared.

"Name and address please." A second officer appeared at my side, ready to write in his notebook.

"El Turner. Parkville Apartments, Apartment 470."

"Can I see some ID?"

"I don't have any on me, officer. Sorry." How stupid of me to have left my purse and phone at home. I stuck my hands in the pockets of my coat, but all I found were my keys and my list of questions. A lot of good they did me now.

"That name sounds familiar."

"I was involved in the Hill House case last year. I know Inspector Poe, ah, I mean Chief of Police Poe."

"I remember that affair. Wasn't there this cute, little, red-haired journalist involved?"

"Yes, Rita Starr. She was my neighbor. We were involved together. I mean we worked on the case together. I don't mean worked, but we were involved," I finished lamely. I couldn't quite make sentences sound normal.

His face harbored a distinct disbelief. I smiled, hoping in his eyes I didn't look like someone who would be selling her wares in that hotel. He wavered, his eyes full of doubt. Should he put a friend of Poe's in handcuffs? Would he get in trouble if he didn't? "Too bad the Chief isn't around to ID you."

"Yes, too bad." If he only knew how much I wished Chief of Police Alan Poe was here.

"Come with me down to the station. This isn't over." He veered on the sign of caution and didn't cuff me, but he did make me ride in the back of the squad car. Bearing the stares of a gathered crowd wasn't a pleasant experience. I could see why some people put their coats over their heads. At least I didn't see anyone taking pictures.

I thought about what my mythical uncle, the dead man, had whispered before he died and decided to keep it to myself for now. I wasn't sure if his words had been meant for me or were just random utterings, but I wanted them to have a meaning, a message, a connection to my mother, whoever she ended up being. Hope is such a human thing.

Chapter 2

At the station, I was grilled over the same issues only from an older, sharper police officer. His eyes held no doubt. He took a report and had me read and sign it. I had one phone call. Poe or Jenny? I called Jenny and left a message.

"Am I under arrest?" I asked.

"Detained for now," came the answer. "Just sit here for the moment."

They kept me in a generic room with a stale cup of coffee for company until they figured out what to do with me. They had taken my coat to test the blood on the sleeve. I played with my keys and went over the list of matters I had wanted to ask a dead man. I tried to understand what had happened. A man who said he was my uncle was now lying in a morgue somewhere. Why had he been killed? Did he know something dangerous? I thought over what he had murmured to me. It had sounded like diamond and Dixie. That made no sense to me. What had he been about to reveal to me about my mother? I thought about our earlier conversation. He indicated I might have information about some merchandise that he could help make disappear. What had he meant by merchandise? Money? Guns? Jewels? Once more, questions swarmed around my head like a thick of bees. As a researcher, I lived in a realm of uncertainties and enjoyed the chase to find answers. This dilemma, however, lingered like a dead man's foul coat. I could see no way of sidestepping the smell.

Before I had been taken into custody, my eyes had done a hurried look around the dead man's room, but I failed to see any documents lying in the open. Maybe the man's come-on was just a ploy to get me to his room. Maybe the mystery woman had taken them. Maybe there was a suitcase still in the closet or under the bed containing fountains of wisdom about my life. Maybe I had been one step away from discovering the real me. Maybe when Poe returned. Maybe.

After another length of tedium, a young officer came into the room, gave me a ticket to reclaim my coat, and took me out. In the hall my neighbor Jenny waited, talking to another woman.

"Oh, El, I'm so glad I got your message. Sorry I could not come sooner. I was at my drum circle." Jenny took the arm of the other woman, a short pear-shaped lady with short gray hair in a stunning white silk pantsuit. "El, this is Charlotte Webb, and she's an attorney. I thought you might need one. She and I are in the same spinning class."

Charlotte held out her hand, giving a light but a bit sticky shake. She turned to the police officer. "Evening, Wilbur. How's the family?"

"Just fine, Ms. Webb."

"So is Ms. Turner being charged with something?"

The officer shook his head. "She was at the scene, had blood on her clothes, and carried no identification. Pretty questionable. Can you verify this is El Turner?"

"Of course, it is! Why didn't you ask Inspector Poe? They are good friends," Jenny cried.

"Jenny, he's at a workshop in DC, and remember

he's Chief of Police Poe now.

"Again, is she being charged with something?" Charlotte interrupted, staring the officer down. "No? Well, then I guess we'll be going, won't we? You know where to find her. Say hello to your wife, Wilbur." She indicated for me to head toward the world outside.

"Just don't leave town, Ms. Turner." He resumed a bit of bravado before the glass doors closed.

We got into her car parked in the lot. "Before we go any further, dear, here is my card with my office and cell numbers. Call if they give you the slightest bit of hassle. And, El, always ask for a lawyer. Never answer questions outside of counsel. Did they read you your rights?"

"I don't think so. They just wanted answers I couldn't give them." I leaned forward. "And I would like to hire you."

We drove in silence to our building. "Before I let you go home, can we have a chat? Maybe in Jenny's apartment?"

Once inside, Jenny ushered us into her office, closed the door, and busied herself making tea. Charlotte took a notebook out of her giant red purse. "Start at the beginning and tell me everything."

I thought back. "Well, I had the impression this guy was following me."

"The deceased?"

"Yes. When I sat down in the park, he plopped down beside me and informed me he was my uncle."

"Your uncle? Didn't you know that?"

"No. You see, my mother when she died said she wasn't my mother, but this man said he knew all about that and would fill me in on who my real mother was."

Charlotte looked a bit confused. Just then Jenny knocked on the door with tea.

"How is everything going?"

"I'm fine, but I think Charlotte needs a bit of history." I took the steaming cup from Jenny.

"I'll fill you in on the back story later, Char," Jenny said. To me she added, "Charlotte is a recent transplant to Parkville."

"Wait," Charlotte said. "Was that the murder of the homeless man? I think I read about that. It was in all the papers."

I nodded. "That was it."

"Don't I also remember something about two women being kidnapped and taken to some dungeon? And there were bank robbers and oodles of stolen money?"

Tired as I was, I had to laugh. "That was me and my neighbor Rita. She is a journalist, but back then she had a very vivid sense of the dramatic."

"But a dungeon?" Charlotte said.

"A creative way of saying basement. Well, it was really a maze of a basement." I took a sip of the tea, hoping it would calm what little shred of nerve I had left. "A dungeon was usually built as some sort of imprisonment."

"But weren't you kept in the dun… ah, basement?"

"Okay." I sighed. "I guess it was a dungeon."

"And on that note, I will leave you two alone." Jenny bowed out.

Charlotte gave me a long look that combined awe and suspicion. "Okay, we'll go from today. This man said he had information about your mother. Did he tell you what it was?"

"He said he was staying at the Grady Hotel and to come in the evening to meet with him."

"Dear, never go anywhere by yourself without telling someone, especially not to that hotel. Mother or not, didn't she ever warn you not to go off to just meet a man?"

"Well, she wasn't exactly an involved parent. There were a lot of different boarding schools and camps and, well, I did leave a message for Jenny, but she wasn't home," I finished weakly. Going into my childhood was not a pleasant excursion. It was a lonely, solitary part of my life I didn't often dwell upon.

"So you went to the hotel," Charlotte continued. "What happened there?"

"I didn't go to the desk since my uncle, the deceased, had given me the room number. I took the stairs and when I opened the door to that floor, this woman barreled into me, almost knocking me down, grabbed my arm to steady herself, and ran down the stairs. I didn't notice the blood she left behind on my jacket until the manager pointed it out later."

"Describe her."

I reiterated what I told the police.

"Do you think you could describe her to a sketch artist?" Charlotte asked.

"Maybe. When I was sitting in the interrogation room, I remembered a bit more about her. At the time, I was just creeped out by the place and anxious to see what the man had to tell me."

"The police are not releasing the name of the deceased until they find out more. What was his name?"

"All he said was to call him Uncle Mickey."

"And you went to his room on that shaky bit of

information? Didn't ask him any questions or get his full name?" She was a breath away from another lecture.

"Stupid, right? It's just that I was anxious to get information about my mother, or non-birth mother, if that's who she was."

"Okay, so you went to the room. Did you knock?"

"I started to but the door was open a bit, so I went in. I walked a few steps and saw his feet sticking out between the two beds. I thought maybe he was ill or had had a heart attack. His coat was thrown over him. There was a knife sticking out of his chest."

"And you touched his coat?"

"Yes, just to lift it up."

"And he was dead?"

"Not at the moment."

Her head shot up, her eyes piercing mine. "What do you mean by that?"

I paused, unsure what to do. Should I tell her?

"Out with it." Those dark eyes bored into mine like a jackhammer.

"Well, he said something that sounded like 'diamond' and then 'Dixie' but that doesn't make any sense. Why would that be someone's last words? I must have misunderstood."

"And it doesn't mean anything to you?"

"Not a thing. That's why I thought I might have misunderstood."

"So, just to get this straight, and please don't be insulted. You didn't have a knife with you, right?"

"Absolutely not."

"What did you do next?"

"At that moment, someone started yelling that I had killed him. The manager came in with a baseball bat.

Then the police filled the room. I wonder now how they got there so fast."

"It seems they were checking an activity on that floor and heard the commotion." She looked at my bobbing head. "I think that's all for now." She got up and opened the office door and called out into the kitchen. "Jenny, I think we should let El go home. El, I'm sure the police will not forget about you. I'll get your number from Jenny in case I need more information. Don't hesitate to call me."

Jenny came back into the room. "Yes, do you want me to help get you settled? Maybe feed and water Albie?"

"I think I'll be all right for now. I just want to shower and get into bed."

"I'll check in on you tomorrow." She saw my look. "But not too early. Shades of Rita!"

We laughed at that. "Char, if you want to stay, I can fill you in on last year in Parkville. If that's okay with you, El."

I nodded wearily then dragged my body home, showered, covered Albie, and flopped into bed. Instead of sugar plums, diamonds danced wickedly through my dreams.

The next morning over coffee, I checked my email. I had cut back on taking clients for genealogical requests, but one or two still filtered in.

****

Dear Ms. Turner:

I emailed you last year about my upcoming wedding and doing horoscopes for the wedding party. BTW they were great! We all loved them. The only problem is that my wife left me. (She said I never did anything right!) I

have gotten behind on my bills and will have to delay my payment to you. I hope that is okay. You are first on my list of people to pay.
　Yours,
　Paul, the future divorcee
****

Email to Paul, the future divorcee
Dear Paul:
I am sorry to hear about your issues, payment and otherwise. While you did initially contact me about the horoscopes, I explained that I work as a genealogist, not an astrologist. You must have found someone who did provide that service. That is the person you should be emailing about payment.
　Best of luck,
　El Turner
****

　Despite all that had happened in the past twenty-four hours, I had to laugh. I guessed I wasn't the only person with problems. Still, it was hard not to get depressed over my own. Just when I thought my life was back on track, I get involved in another murder. I couldn't even blame this one on Rita! The hands of my mother, or possible so-called one, were reaching out for me from the grave, and I didn't like it. Why had the dead man contacted me now, and why in the world had he spouted the words 'Dixie' and 'diamond' to me? That is, if I heard good old Uncle Mickey correctly. I wish he had instead used his last dying energy to point to a file lying nearby that contained all the answers to my life. Somehow, I imagined the wholesome town of Parkville to be one of peace and comfort, not one of murder. Had I somehow brought a curse to this poor place? Or was my mother having one more laugh at my expense?

Finally, my brain stopped its memory lane dawdle and kicked into gear. I hit the computer and started searches for Mick Taylor, Mickey Taylor, Michael Taylor. It got me nowhere. None of the images looked like him, and there were way too many to go mad dashing. Could I even really trust that that was his real name? If he was anything like my mother, his real name would be long forgotten. Next, I tried Elizabeth Taylor, Lizzie Taylor, Liz Taylor, but, again, a fool's journey. All roads led to the movie star. I tried diamond and Dixie. That resulted in about twenty-seven million hits. Dixie and diamond resulted in less, only eight million hits. I stopped and shook my head.

What was wrong with me? I was a researcher who should know better, not some college freshman unused to finding information. Some people liked crosswords or jigsaw puzzles, but I liked solving other problems. Now, however, I had once more surrendered to brain fog. I decided a walk was in order to clear my head of past happenings.

I set out for Sherman Park, again hoping to see my old friend Will Pepper. I hadn't gone far before I heard his raspy voice.

"Hey, girlie, aren't you in the wrong park?"

I looked over at the bench where the silver-haired gent was mixing it up with other old veterans. "Hey, Sarge! You're just the man I was looking for."

"Hear that, fellas? You'll have to excuse me. It's not every day that a pretty young woman wants my company." He stood up and walked over, pointing to a bench well out of earshot. I forgot how tall he was, his shadow making my five foot five frame seem a lot smaller.

"How have you been, Sarge? It's good to see you again."

"Just fine. And you? If all those newspaper stories were even partly true, it seems you and your reporter friend went through some tough times last year, but you caught some bad guys, solved a murder, found a ton of stolen money, and got this town headed in the right direction. Sounds like something out of a book."

"It certainly was a strange situation."

"Ha! Strange is hardly the word for it. You sure did something for this town by finding Clark Hill's old journal. Proved our town founder was a good guy at that. Guess all those old rumors about him were just that." He slapped his knee. "Why, our opportunistic mayor can't get his picture in the paper often enough—renaming Main Street as Clark Hill Street, christening a new building as Clark Hill Hall. I suppose a statue will be next or a town parade."

"I'm just glad Clark Hill has his good name restored."

"Hey, I went to that exhibit at the library where copies of some pages from his journal were displayed. Sure was quite a spectacle. All those folks falling over themselves trying to say they were a distant relative of Mr. Hill."

"The town has established a historical society to handle all the items folks have suddenly found in their attics and basements relating to Clark Hill. Guess it's safe to bring them out now. The society is renting a temporary building downtown."

"Say, whatever happened to all that stolen money the robbers hid in the Hill House? Did you and your friend get a reward?"

"Well, the money went back to the bank the robbers took it from. Rita and I donated the reward money we got to the historical society I just mentioned. Since the old Hill House has been abandoned for years and used for nefarious purposes, let's say, Parkville leaders took possession. They are going to fix it up as an actual home for the journal and all the other artifacts and call it a museum. People are donating time, and businesses are offering supplies to help. I think the mayor is hoping it will become a tourist attraction."

"Whee, girlie! For someone who blew into this town not knowing a thing about us, you done all right. Say, they ought to make you head of that society."

"They did ask, and, believe me, it would be great fun to see what's in that old house, but I have another project to tackle. With all my memories about being locked in that basement and having guns aimed at me, I'm not sure I want to go back in that house for a while."

"Don't blame you at all."

"I want to put all that behind me now." I smiled and closed my eyes to the sun, only half believing my words.

I heard his soft chuckle. "Spring sure is a fine time for romance, don't you think?"

I turned to look at him. "What have you heard?"

He switched up the subject. "Heard tell this town got a new murder happening." He cleared his throat. "Wouldn't know anything about that, would you?"

"Don't ask," I sighed.

"El, you're like that woman on the TV, that teacher who finds a dead body everywhere she goes."

"Oh, man, I hope that doesn't happen to me."

"So, you need my help with something?"

"Well, I hit a wall in my research and thought some fresh air would flush out this thing I like to call a brain."

"Throw something out at me and let's see what sticks."

"Okay. Do the words 'Dixie' and 'diamond' mean anything to you?"

He thought for a moment. "Funny you should ask. During the war, we had a USO show featuring some fan dancers called the Dixie Diamonds. I think they were from Alabama or Georgia. Anyway, they had these gigantic pink feathered things, and we weren't exactly sure what they were wearing behind those fans. Most of us hoped it was nothing!"

"Well, this is a new side to you, Sarge."

"Oops, guess I shouldn't have gotten so racy. Am I blushing?"

We both laughed, and it felt good to be in the light and talk about things other than dead uncles and mysterious mothers.

****

Talking to Will Pepper ignited a few ideas in my sorry brain. I hadn't thought about the words being the name of a group. I wondered if my mother had been a fan dancer. I tried to remember if Uncle Mickey had said diamond first or Dixie. And had he used the plurals diamonds and Dixies? I had been too stunned to remember. When I got home, I tried a better search tactic.

Dixie Diamonds led to sites about a hot country singing duo, a glitzy yoyo company, a famous airplane that was lost at sea, and recipes for a newly discovered southern pepper. When I switched things up and tried Diamond Dixies, there were sites for a senior women's barbershop quartet, an antique store run by sisters, a new ice cream bar, and a website for strippers with most of the pictures blacked out, but nothing to match what I wanted. What did I want? Something that made sense. A trip to the library was in order.

I knocked on Jenny's door before I left and told her where I was going. I knew her canasta group met on that day, but it seemed like she was staying home to keep a watch on me.

"Perhaps you should wait until Inspector Poe gets back before you venture out into the world," she said, rain-in-the-forest music filling the air behind her. "I saw you went out this morning without telling me." She waved a warning finger at me. "Do you want me to go along with you? My car's full of gas and ready to hit the road."

"Thank you for the offer, Jenny, but I fear it will be a boring outing. I'll be careful. I promise. It's just a quick trip to the library and back." I tried to smile convincingly. "And I guess we might have to get used to calling him Chief of Police Poe."

"That won't be as easy as it sounds." She chuckled. "Well, I'll be here if you need me, El. My phone is on."

Just as I turned toward the elevators, I saw a movement out of the corner of my eye. A woman was coming out of Rita's apartment. It took a minute before I remembered it wasn't Rita's apartment anymore. Someone else must have moved in. As I was staring at the woman, she turned and headed rapidly my way, a huge smile on her face.

"Oh, hi! You must be El. My cousin told me so much about you, I feel like I know you already."

The force with which she was descending on me as

well as the word cousin sent chills through my body recalling the recent dead uncle episode. With only a second to debate whether to run or try to get back into my apartment, I found myself face to face with the young woman.

"Can I hug you?"

I must have appeared shocked because she backed off instantly. I realized I had raised my hands out in front of me as protection.

"Sorry. I didn't mean to startle you." The smile stayed plastered on her face as she examined me like a specimen in a laboratory. Her eagerness hung in the air like party balloons.

When I didn't say anything, she continued, "Well, excuse my lack of manners. I'm Dolly Davis." Seeing no reaction, she tried again. "I think you know my cousin, Ida. She works at the library."

Finally, some sense of reality drilled through my bewilderment. "Ida Parks?"

"Yes. She's my cousin. I guess from your look, she told me more about you than she told you about me. I'm new to Parkville. Maybe we better start over. Hi. I'm Dolly Davis."

"Hi, Dolly. Sorry to be so scattered, but odd things have been happening to me lately. It's nice to meet you." I considered the woman before me. Where Ida Parks was older, chic, and professional in dress, Dolly was a crazy mix of off-the-shoulder pink blouse and patchwork bib overhauls that seemed several sizes too big; where Ida's hair was sleek and pulled back, Dolly's head contained a tumbled mass of dark tight curls; and where Ida maintained a reserved, helpful face, Dolly's was raw excitement. "I think Ida did tell me about you. I'm just a bit forgetful. In fact, I was on my way to the library to do some research. Are you headed in that direction?"

"I don't mean to hold you up," she said, smile ever present. "I'm on my way out of town. Got a gig tonight."

I noticed she was pulling a suitcase on wheels. I mused over the name. "Dolly? Does that mean you're a singer?"

Her laugh twisted into a sad chuckle. "My name is Dolly Loretta Davis. Does that give you an indication of what kind of music my mother loved? Twelve years of singing lessons and a lot of her prayers didn't pave the way in that direction. I made her cry when I decided to be a standup comedian. You have to follow your heart, right? I go by Dolly Dee when I'm on stage."

"I totally agree about following your heart. Again, it's nice to meet you, Dolly. If there's anything I can do to help you settle in, please let me know." It's a comment people throw off not expecting or hoping for an answer.

She paused for a second. "Well, I hate to ask it. I'll be gone for over a week, and I have a bunch of boxes still to unpack, but if you could just check on Spike and Agnes, I'd appreciate it."

What had my big mouth gotten me into? Please don't let it be animals of any kind, I silently begged, and please no snakes. "Who and who?"

"Spike and Agnes, my cacti. Spike is an old man cactus, and Agnes is an old lady cactus. They don't need water or anything, but they do like the sound of a human voice now and then. I baby them too much, so they miss me when I'm on the road."

I didn't know what to make of this revelation and could do little more than stammer an okay.

"Oh, I am so late. Here's my extra key. Thank you

so much. Say hello to Cousin Ida for me. Tell her I got here safely." She thrust a shiny object at me, checked her watch, and flew off toward the elevators. I watched her go then leaned against the wall, sure I had been in a hurricane or storm of some sort.

When I figured she was out of the building, I took a slow walk down the stairs just to be sure. The encounter was still processing in my brain. Ida had never mentioned a cousin or any family member that I could recall. She usually presented a private demeanor. At least the meeting had, for the moment, taken my mind off my present problems. I desperately needed a cone of safety, and the library provided that. Ida Parks, the tall, statuesque woman who oversaw the place, was a kindred spirit in more ways than one. Her mother had named her hoping for an activist; my mother named me hoping for a movie star. Both of us had dashed those hopes. Now it seemed like another daughter had sent a mother's dreams hurtling toward the abyss.

Chapter 3

The library had digitalized many of their records and had access to several large newspaper archives. I hoped to find something, a doorway perhaps, that made sense of my mother and her secrets. Those secrets could go a long way into explaining what tie we shared, if any. If there was no link, how had we come to be a family? And why had she chosen to tell me the truth after she died? Her letter the lawyer Mason Street had given me at the cemetery was burned into my brain: *I'm not your mother.* It had been the last thing I expected and the worst thing in my life to date. What purpose did that serve except to turn my whole existence upside down? Had she been just plain mean or way too guilty?

My birth certificate, real or not, listed Los Angeles as my city of birth, so I started there, trying Dixie Diamonds and Los Angeles. Of course, being LA, diamonds popped up like rabid dandelions. The newspapers were ensconced in diamonds. I couldn't steer away from the glittering references: celebrities, sales, weddings, the Four Cs. Not to mention all the colors: champagne, lemonade, chocolate, cognac. I couldn't decide if I was getting hungry or thirsty. Then I hit the pink diamonds. For a solid hour, I fell under the spell of the faint, the fancy, the vivid pinks, and I understood what might have captivated my mother. Finally, I looked away from the computer screen, blinked my eyes, and morphed into the researcher once more, steering wide of the wink and luster.

After much misdirection, one link led me to a decades-past jewelry heist by a group of old women. That let my mother out. Or did it? The event felt like a spark, some off-the-wall association, had been made in my brain to a memory I couldn't quite recall. I sat back and tried to make that leap, but the thread was gone like cloud fluff on a breezy day. Out of the corner of my eye, I saw Ida passing by.

"And what are you intensely trying to ponder?" She peered over the red glasses on her nose.

"Just trying to fit my mother into a slot marked criminal."

"From what you've told me, it sure doesn't sound like her. Are you trying to find information about her or are you making a joke?"

"I'm trying to track down a reference to either Diamond Dixies or Dixie Diamonds, although I have no idea what they might refer to."

"Doesn't ring a bell for me either. Sorry."

"Do you know much about diamonds?"

"Only what's on my finger." She held her hand out with a small ring showing. "It's all the mister could afford when we got married, but I love it just the same."

"It's beautiful, Ida, and the sentiment outweighs the carats."

"Going on thirty years. He's often mentioned getting me a bigger stone, but I'm not interested." She stared lovingly at the ring.

"Congratulations on a happy marriage, Ida, and before I forget, congratulations also on being named to the Board of the Parkville Historical Society! I have been meaning to come by and say how proud I am of you."

"It's all your doing, El. You and your friend Rita helped get it started when you donated your reward money from those robberies last year. We have a building we are using until we can move into the Hill House. There's a lot to fix in that house, so it might be a while. For right now, we are sorting through pictures, letters, all sorts of things people have been bringing in that might be related to Clark Hill and early Parkville. It appears the state has finally taken an interest in our town's history. We are still waiting on the state archivist for release of Clark's journal, the one you found in that basement when you were kidnapped." She gave a shudder. "I don't know how you two survived all that turmoil."

"Well, at that time, Rita's middle name was drama."

We both laughed. A nearby library patron gave us an evil eye shush, so we quieted down to silent giggles.

"You should come by," Ida said in her library voice. "Your name always comes up as someone who should be a board member. At least have an active part in what we are doing. You're the research expert."

"Thanks, Ida. I'll try to come by one day. Right now, I've got a big project to finish."

"Oh, guess what. Our friends Cassandra Troy and Senor Marquez have been named to the board as well. You wouldn't believe how Cassie has changed. After years of trying to convince the town that Clark Hill was not guilty of all the rumors that were spread about him, she is finally in her glory. He was the great man she always said he was. Several people have volunteered to help her go through her house to see what she has hidden away that might have historical significance."

"How wonderful! I must admit Cassie scared me when I first met her. She was one step away from crazy. Glad to see she is on the right path. However, I don't think I will ever forgive you for not letting me know about her in advance. That first trip to her house keeps showing up in my nightmares." I smiled at the memory.

"Totally my fault. It was a bad trick on my part, and one I have been sorry for ever since."

"Hmmm. That may be, but I happened to come across another example of what you are not telling me."

"And that would be?"

"Does Cousin Dolly ring any bells?"

"Dolly? Where in the world did you come across her?" Ida looked startled.

"In my building. It seems she's moved into Rita's old apartment, just down the hall from me."

"What? Something is not computing here. And she wasn't supposed to be here for another few months. I never imagined you two would meet up like that." She looked me over to gauge my mood. "It seems I owe you another apology. Sorry."

"I don't remember you ever mentioning her."

"I don't think I have. She's somewhat… alternative. Her mother is heartbroken at her choice of career. I think she urged Dolly to move here hoping I would talk her out of being a comedian. She was always a funny girl growing up, making jokes, putting on plays, that sort of thing. I never believed she'd try to make a career out of it."

"I got a healthy slice of her life." I smiled to ease the tension I saw build up in Ida. "At least what she could tell me in the five minutes of our meeting. She's very energetic. How does she know so much about me? What did you tell her?"

"For a gal who devours newspapers, you should know their reach and power to inform. You do remember you made all the headlines last year, don't you? Woman who saved the town."

"I'm trying to block it out. Sorry. Anyway, she's in the building."

"The last I heard, she and a handful of other touring comedians were going to rent a place to use as their base of operations." She shook her head and looked my way. "And now she's in your building. All I can say is she's harmless though very excitable. Youth has its own energy. At least she's on the road a lot."

"Excitable, yes. She's already given me the key to her place to talk to her cactus plants."

"Oh, goodness. Does she still have those mangy things? I'll try to tap into the family line tonight and see what's up. Please don't feel obligated. You can give me the key if you want."

"That's okay. I talk to my bird all the time. I guess I can manage a few words to a pair of cacti. It will give me a break from research."

Ida cocked her dark head and gave me a sideways look. "Honey, you might have told me at one time, but how in the world did you ever end up being a genealogist?"

"I don't really know, Ida." I shrugged.

"There must have been something that led you in this direction," she prodded. "When your third-grade teacher asked you what you wanted to be when you grew up, did you say genealogist?" She sat down beside me.

"Now that's funny, Ida. Thanks, I needed another good laugh." I put my elbows on the table and thought for a moment. "I'm not sure there was an ah-ha event, but maybe my childhood guided me in that direction."

"How so?"

"Well, I think I told you that we moved around a lot. Because of that I was never in any one school for long, and half the time my mother taught me at home."

"Was she a teacher?"

"No, but she always had a few textbooks on hand. Who knows where she got them, but one month we'd study history, then the next math. She'd give me these worksheets she made up with questions, and I would have until the end of the week to search the books and find the answers. She'd tear out the index pages and table of contents so I really had to look hard. She'd give me a grade, and if I kept my average up, at the end of that month, she'd take me to a library and let me check out two books as a reward. I could wander around as long as I wanted until I decided. Sometimes she would drop me off for an afternoon. Then I'd find my books and spend the rest of the time reading ones I didn't check out. I'd find a corner and just snuggle in for a few hours. Usually though she would sit outside with a coffee, a cigarette, and her notebook." A dash of memories suddenly flooded my mind.

"What was that?" Ida asked. "You looked like you just got a shock."

"Just some odd recollections keep popping up. And a lot of questions to go with them. It's a bit like living in a quiz show and the clock is ticking."

"Well, I better let you get back to your search. Good luck, honey. Hope you find the answers you're seeking."

She wasn't the only one.

****

I didn't mention it to Ida, but my mother's notebooks had now moved to the front of the line in my brain. It's hard to know how many years I spent not thinking about her, about that part of my life; now it was all I could think about. So many images had lately flooded my mind about my mother, always with a notebook not far from her hand. There was one time I got curious. She had left a notebook out on our kitchen table, and I sat in her chair and began to go through the pages. Each page seemed to contain a drawing of some sort, lines with measurements, illustrations of doors and exits, calculations of timetables. Nothing had made much sense at the time. I had gone to get my colored pencils and decided to add a drawing of my own to the pages. When she returned, she had become volatile, grabbing the book and yelling that if I ever, ever, ever touched one of her notebooks again, she'd make sure I couldn't sit down for a year. There had been no notebooks in the few boxes of her personal items I found after her death. Had they been hidden? Was there another golden horde of information stuffed away somewhere else? Or had they all been destroyed by her paranoia?

I told myself I was being silly, but the drawings now seemed to have an illegal edge to them. What had she been involved in? On a whim, I tried searching for Diamond Dixies and robberies, Diamond Dixies and jewels, and Diamond Dixies and heists. Then with the terms reversed. Not a lot of information was available pre-internet. Newspapers, especially smaller ones, were not often aware of what was happening in other distant areas of the country.

Then I happened upon an article by an enterprising young journalist for a middling newspaper. *Do you know where your wife was last night? Could she be a Diamond Dixie?* Read the headline. The article referenced a random paper in Iowa that reported the robbery of a local jeweler who claimed "two good-looking dames with Southern accents" had been behind it. "They just wanted diamonds," he had said. "Those damn Diamond Dixies took all I had." The line struck a funny bone with the journalist.

His piece was a humorous one, fanning the issue of women's activism of the 1970s. He seemed to laugh at the very idea that not only could women be out working or protesting, but now also robbing jewelry stores. The article made light of even the suggestion that women could be that smart and organized to execute a robbery, much less get away with it. He was convinced it had been men dressed up as women and using fake accents. The article had been syndicated in several places.

A few weeks later, a follow up appeared: *Diamond Dixie Mania?* The journalist was back, indicating that a small flurry of reports had come in to his newspaper from all over the country about heists involving women. He insisted he had been making a joke of the matter and again repeated that such a feat was beyond the capability of women. Kitchens and bedrooms were prominently mentioned. The reported robberies were probably a result of his article, he stated, and the women involved would soon be caught. A cartoon showing a grandmother robbing a jewelry store while holding a carrot like a gun appeared next to the article.

For some reason, that joggled a memory about carrots that I couldn't quite place. My brain had built a fuzzy lint warehouse inside my skull and visited it whenever it wanted to, hand picking recollections off the shelves. Why could I remember some things and not others? For all the years spent with my mother, I had never questioned her work or her absences. She told me she worked in the insurance industry and had to travel a lot. I had carried a child's faith of innocence.

I thanked whatever search muses produced enterprising young journalists and made note of the original robbery with the older women and the two random reports he had mentioned. I made copies and trucked on.

Going deeper into the world of theft, I found a small string of robberies during the 80s and the 90s. Nothing seemed connected. They all had different descriptions of the robbers and none of the situations was the same, but they formed a diamond pattern for me. The offenders were all women. In one, a woman in a wheelchair came in with her nurse. The elderly woman developed stomach pains and had to be hurried out, supposedly to a hospital. In another, two wealthy-looking women came in and distracted the one clerk on duty before hurrying out to a late lunch date they had forgotten. Another recounted how a rich middle-aged woman was shopping when a poor homeless person wandered in and caused a scene, and the shoppers ran out. In all instances, jewelry was missing afterward. Police weren't convinced the robberies were done by the same people, making it hard for them to trace. The internet hadn't really been born yet.

In the early 1990s, an article revealed a robbery where a child was involved. A young woman had entered the store and begun looking at necklaces. She had troubled the salesclerk for a glass of water for her child when the child suddenly started throwing up all over the place. Since it was a reputable business, the clerk quickly tried to clean up the mess, with the woman helping and extremely sorry, then whisking her child out of the store. It wasn't until later he discovered the missing items. He thought in all the fuss, the woman had taken them by mistake, and the store was waiting for her to return them. I guess it was a long wait.

Reports indicated jewelry of all sorts taken, but the predominant items were diamonds. Once or twice a writer brought up the Diamond Dixies, but the term faded as quickly as it had arisen. Since few people carried cell phones back then and smaller stores rarely had video cameras, no pictures of the suspects were available. In several instances, police had commissioned sketch artists, but none of the drawings matched. Police thought the suspects may have used disguises or been local pranksters. When the sketched pictures were shown to the victims, they failed to recognize anyone. Police never had any suspects or even leads. Since the women often wore gloves, fingerprints were nonexistent. Heists happened all over the country, often at smaller jewelers, sometimes museums, sometimes malls. No cars were ever seen nor license numbers recorded. Reports were meager and sketchy. The articles always ended with the police asking the public's help for information. None appeared to have been solved, and larger issues always dominated the news.

My head was spinning. Was I on the trail of my mother's history or just a random goose chase? I wondered if the woman in the hallway of the Grady Hotel had been involved in some way. A sudden thought zipped through my brain like a lightning bolt: Had I been the small child? Had my mother used me in her schemes?

My brain scoffed at the very idea, but now I advanced my thinking from laughter to serious consideration of my mother's activities. In reality, the possibilities appeared shaky, totally absurd. Yes, my mother had been secretive and distant, but a jewel thief? The truth appeared to be a rapid, wavering line I couldn't quiet, but things just seemed to be falling into place where I had least expected them to drop. It was a feeling I often got when my researcher instincts began to take on a bloodhound scent. This development might account for Uncle Mickey's offer of help to get rid of the "merchandise," as he had put it. What merchandise? Jewels? If so, I had no clue where they might be. Nothing my mother left behind pointed in that direction. I had never seen a diamond. She didn't even wear a watch.

"This is making my head hurt," I said out loud, forgetting where I was. The evil-eyed shusher looked ready to dial 911, so I hastily gathered my meager bundle to read at home. Half of me discarded the silly notion of my mother being involved in some crime wave; the other half felt distinctly uneasy. I wasn't sure I was ready to discover my history. The police already had me in their sights.

****

Email to El Turner
Dear El Turner:

Could you please find my aunt? I lost her in Paris 20 years ago, and I have not been able to find her since. Will you see what you can do? Her name was Wilma Stone. I am not sure if she ever married. Are you taking on new clients?

Thanks,
Hannah B.

****

Email to Hannah B.

Dear Hannah:

Thank you for your email. I'm not exactly sure what you want me to do. Do you need a detective for a present-day search or are you looking for her history? A marriage or death certificate? I would be happy to help if you would give me a bit more specifics. Do you have her birth certificate or that information? Can you give me her place of birth and her journey to Paris? And, yes, I am taking on a few clients at present. My rates are enclosed as well as payment information.

Best,
El Turner

****

Email to El Turner

I'm so sorry! You must think I'm an idiot. I meant to say I lost my aunt's trail as I was doing my family tree. At least, I think it was her. I found a death certificate with Wilhelmina Stone there and wonder if it was her. I've enclosed the information you requested as well as a list of documents I could not find. Any help is much appreciated. My father always said she was an odd duck in our family. He always thought she died years earlier, but nothing much was known about her. My father lost touch with her decades ago. As far as we know, she lived alone and never married. He said she had been very religious, even as a child, and left home when she was 17 or 18. She just packed a small suitcase and left a note for her parents. She had no friends, so no one knew where she had gone. As I said, I think I found her in Paris, but could find nothing before that. Money sent to your account. Go until it is used up. Please email or text

Allison Thorpe

if you have questions.
 Thanks,
 Hannah B.

Chapter 4

I knocked on Jenny's door and let her know I had gotten home safely and would be staying in, so she could go to her book club meeting. I unlocked my apartment and headed straight for my parrot's cage. My sounding board and therapist was napping. I had a lot to unload on him at present.

"Oh, Albie. I'm not sure I like where this limb of my family tree is taking me. Do you think my mother could have been involved in robbery? Was that the secret Uncle Mickey was going to tell me?"

I dumped the printouts from my morning efforts on the desk. Since Poe had started spending more time in my apartment and sharing dinners, I had moved my computer and papers to the second bedroom. Before, I had set up command central of family trees on my kitchen table, papers and scribblings covering the whole top. I had always kept the door of the other bedroom closed on the few boxes of my mother's things gathered after her death, not wanting to delve into their riddles at that time. Covering them with a variety of clever disguises like a jacket or a towel hadn't worked; they had always declared their presence. Now they occupied a corner of my new office and caught my eye every time I sat down at my desk. At least I had finally opened them and made a cursory exploration. Not much had leapt out and spoken to me. A search on that family tree would have to be done by instinct alone. What kind of family offers no documentation? No Bible full of births and death? No handwritten tales of ancestry? Answer: Mine.

I gave Albie a treat and changed his water. "Albie, I hate to admit it, but I think my mother might have been a jewel thief."

"Thief!" Albie echoed, more concerned with the goodie he was attacking.

I wondered at my decision to research my family tree. Was I prepared for what I might find? I could handle any facts about lives I uncovered for other people, but this was different. My life had gone along just fine. I had spent most of my life thinking the woman I had buried was my mother. Drat the woman for telling me differently. And why was I willing to dig up secrets I might not want to know, either about my so-called mother or about myself? It was amazing how much of my life I had tucked away and never examined. I wondered if I had a real mother out there somewhere. If so, had she worried about me all these years? Had she cried herself to sleep when I went missing? Had she kept my room as it was on the day I disappeared? Brush and mirror on top of the wood dresser? Stuffed animals on the bed? Did I have a doll? My head started throbbing again. How much time had I spent recently asking the same questions? Beating my head against the wall might have been easier. Well, I was into it now. The growing urge to know overrode the fear of what I might uncover.

I now could clearly understand the anxiety and bravery folks felt when digging into their lineage. I vowed to treat the facts I found for clients in future requests, good or bad, with a much gentler approach. It was scary territory.

Reaching for the few article copies, I scanned them again with no greater insight. I went to the computer and tried various other searches with no luck. It seemed none of the robbery incidents were high profile cases. There had to be other approaches to this mystery.

Later in the evening, Poe phoned.

"How's everything going?"

"Just fine. How's the seminar?"

"Interesting. It just shows how far behind the curve we are in Parkville."

It was a normal chat until he was about to hang up.

"By the way, El, I don't know if you've heard or not, but a man was murdered in the Grady Hotel."

I paused too long.

"Please don't tell me."

I had wanted to tell him about the ugly news in person. "It's a long story. I'm sure you will hear all about it when you get back."

He paused. "Sergeant Little said a woman had been brought in for questioning. That wouldn't have been you, would it?" I could hear his voice rising.

I think he heard my gulp across the phone lines.

"Oh, El." I could feel the steam emanating from the phone.

"Listen, before you fly off the handle, I did not kill the man. I was just in the wrong place at the wrong time."

"What in the world were you doing at the Grady Hotel in the middle of the night? Don't you know what kind of place that is?"

"First of all, it wasn't the middle of the night, and second, the man said he had information about my mother. He told me he was my Uncle Mickey."

The line was quiet for a moment. "Are you sure he

wasn't trying to capitalize on last year's events?"

"I thought of that. I had a plan all set out."

"Yeah, I know about your plans. I'm sure you also had backup with you or at least told someone where you were going?

"Listen, I'll tell you all about it when you get home. Jenny has a friend who is a lawyer, and I've hired her, so I'm covered. Just enjoy the seminar."

"El, I'd gotten tired of telling you this last year, but please stay inside. Don't get into any more trouble. Stay home and let the police handle it. I know I sound like an old thirty-three record stuck in a groove. Who knew genealogy was such a dangerous profession? You should have warned me."

"You just worry too much. I'm fine. Just went to the library to see Ida today. Very innocent. Believe me, I don't want any trouble."

"Well, see that you and Albie stay out of this one."

"I'll try."

But I was already planning my trip for the morning. What harm could that do?

****

The Grady Hotel wasn't much better in daylight hours. I hoped the manager was around; I wanted to get some answers. I didn't know if he would recognize me or not, so I put on a floppy sun hat Rita had left behind and big round sunglasses. Poe would have my socks and wring them around my neck for doing this. I had even snuck out on Jenny. I knew I was taking chances, but this was my life. I had to follow all the leads. My restless quest to know my origins kept overriding any common sense left in my body.

A stout friendly woman with an off-center wig was

at the front desk. "Checking in?" Her voice echoed with good cheer and delight.

"No. I'd like to speak with the manager if he's in."

"Oh, you must be from the newspaper." I thought she might jump up and down with joy. "They said someone was coming by today to do a story."

I took a notebook and pen from my bag and tried to look professional. She gestured for me to follow her into the back room. I kept my sunglasses and hat on. The manager sat behind a cluttered desk working on some kind of ledger.

"Someone to see you," she said and left.

He looked up and saw the notebook and pen in my hand. "Oh, the press." He ran a hand through greasy wisps of hair, trying to slick them down. "Welcome. Have a seat."

I tried to find one that didn't look like it had come from the Titanic. "I have a few questions if you have time." I tried not to look him in the eye.

"Anything for the press." He leaned back and put his hands behind his head.

"Can you give me the name of the man who was killed?"

"Didn't you get that from the police?" he asked. "Surely they have it."

"Just trying to make sure it is correct. Double checking my sources." I hoped my briskness would come off as professional.

"He wrote his name down as Mick Taylor."

"I also want to ask when he registered and where he was from."

The manager was giving me a more intense stare.

"Sometimes the police take the information down

wrong." I shrugged, trying to make it sound like this happened to reporters every day of the week.

"All he wrote in the ledger was New York. Said he was here on business. The jewelry business, I think." He took his hands from behind his head and leaned his arms on the desk, revealing what could have been a wink or an eye tic.

"When exactly did he register?" I smiled sweetly in case he had winked, hoping to wring all the information I could from him.

"You look familiar. Have we met?" His words screeched my heart to a standstill.

I kept my head down and wrote furiously. "Did he check in alone? A person I talked to at the police station said he checked in with a woman."

He paused for a breathless second. "No. He checked in alone. Although a woman did visit him. She asked me what room he was in. I heard them arguing a few times. On the day he died, in fact."

"Can you describe her?" I imagined the manager was the sort to creep along the hallways and listen in on conversations.

"Probably a fox in her day, but long in the tooth now. Dyed hair. Wore a baseball hat. Sunglasses. Tried to hide her appearance."

He stood up suddenly and pointed his finger at me. "Hey, you're the lady that killed him!" His face took on a red tinge as he grew angry. "I thought you were in jail. How dare you come here and question me! Get out before I call the police for harassing me." I saw his baseball bat in the corner.

I grabbed my stuff and ran out; the woman at the desk had a shocked look on her happy face.

I broke speed records getting home, then settled behind my desk, trying to persuade the world I had been there all along. The rest of the day was spent innocently doing research on Hannah B's aunt, Wilma Stone. Today, I wished I could disappear to Paris as she had done.

****

Poe was furious when he called that night. "El, I'm not sure I can go through this again with you. Do I have to put you in jail to keep you safe?" The phone felt like a red-hot poker against my ear.

"You know how I am." I tried a soft puppy dog voice.

"Won't work, El. That man could be a suspect in a murder."

"He's a suspect! I knew it! What's the motive?"

"I said *could* be."

"Well, when I was going to the hotel room to see Uncle Mickey, there was a woman who bumped into me in the hall and then ran away. The manager told me she had been in my uncle's room several times, and they had argued on the day he was killed. Has anyone seen her? Are you following leads?"

"Whoa, Tiger. Did he describe her?"

"Just an older woman, maybe 60s, dyed dark hair, baseball hat. I think she might have been part of the Diamo—" My tongue braked with a shrieking halt. I had not told Poe about what Uncle Mickey had said or about my research. I wanted to be the one to solve the case or at least provide some important clues. I wanted him to know I had skills beyond punching keys on a computer.

"Dia who?"

I scrambled for a response. Poe knew me too well.

"He thought her name might be Diane or Dinah. He wasn't sure."

"So, I suppose you've already done research on Uncle Mickey, huh? Did he give you a last name?"

"I think he said Taylor," I hedged.

He switched topics and brought up the elephant in my life. "Had a chance to go through those boxes from your mother yet? Did she ever mention an uncle to you? Maybe there is something there about her family. You need to stay at home and search whatever she left behind."

"I've gone through a bit," I offered, glad for the subject change. "But there's not much there. The woman was a mystery. Some old receipts to who knows where. She blacked out a lot of information on anything that might be of use. Who does that? But she had a receipt for every month over a year from the same place." I hadn't done more than open the boxes and peek inside. "I've been too busy with other research to dig deeper."

"Research having to do with this case?"

"I do have a job, you know. And I really must get back to it." I pretended to sound offended.

"I thought you were not taking on any more research jobs so you could delve into your own family tree. Am I wrong, or was that the plan?"

"It still is the plan. I just took a few of the more challenging ones to keep me sharp." In truth, I wasn't sure if I agreed to the requests in order to keep sharp or to avoid looking into my own life. I certainly didn't need the income. Before my mother begged me to come to Parkville to take care of her, I had a very lucrative job researching for a television show. The work sent me all over the country with healthy travel expenses and nice hotels. When my mother died, I had stayed in Parkville, letting the fat bank account see me through the off times.

"Okay, but you have been warned, El. I'm serious." My mind snapped back to Poe.

"Yes, sir. See you soon."

"You can count on it."

Just to show I hadn't lied, I did another half-hearted search through the boxes. Still no notebooks or pages from notebooks. No mention of family. No work history. What had the woman been up to? When I satisfied myself that I could give a better report to Poe, I went back to my computer and the Diamond Dixies.

****

"Seems the police want to have another chat," Charlotte Webb said over the phone the next day. "I think they also had a complaint from the manager of the Grady Hotel against you. Did you really go to see him and pretend to be a reporter?"

"Ms. Webb, I didn't say I was a reporter. I just wanted to get a few things straight. He saw my notepad and assumed. I didn't correct him." I tried to sound convincing.

"Hmmm. Well, whatever the case, can you meet me at police headquarters at two? I should be out of court by then."

"Yes, ma'am," I said.

"By the way, forget the ma'am and Ms. Webb stuff and just call me Charlotte. I feel old as Circe as it is."

"Will do," I said but she had already hung up.

I knew Poe was back and wondered if he would be there.

Two o'clock came, but Poe was not in the small room with the police detective Joe Munday, Charlotte, and me. He had to be watching or listening somewhere.

The detective had a low, rough voice. "We have a complaint from Hy Sheldon saying that you were harassing him."

"Hy who?" Was there someone else with a complaint against me? Maybe I should be keeping track.

"Hyatt Sheldon, the manager of the Grady Hotel. He said you pretended to be a reporter to gain access to his office."

Charlotte put her hand on my arm and shook her head. "Ms. Turner went to the hotel to ask Mr. Sheldon a few innocent questions. She had a pad of paper and a pen. She never said she was from the press. It's not her fault if Mr. Sheldon made that assumption."

"Let's put that aside for now. I would caution you not to go back. We might view the next time as harassment."

"Are you barring her from visiting the hotel again, Detective Munday?" Charlotte asked.

"It's just a caution, Ms. Webb. Now then, Ms. Turner, have you thought of anything else you have not told us?"

I turned to Charlotte who nodded.

"Well, I moved to Parkville several years ago to take care of my mother, Lizzie Turner. When she died, I stayed on. Her house was rented, and she had few possessions. At her burial, she sent a note through Mason Street that she was not my real mother. When the dead man showed up, he told me he was my Uncle Mickey, my mother's brother Mickey Taylor. He said her real name was Lizzie Taylor, and he knew who my birth mother was. He said he would tell me if I went to his hotel room that night at the Grady. He gave me the room number. No one was at the desk, so I took the stairs. As I walked out into the hallway, a woman in a baseball hat, dark hair, and sunglasses knocked into me. She grabbed my arm. When I got to his room, the door was open a bit, so I went in. I saw him lying between the beds. His heavy overcoat was covering him. When I pulled it back, I saw he had been stabbed." I hesitated.

"My report says you didn't touch anything." He stared into my eyes.

"I thought the officer meant in the room or on the table. I just pulled the coat back a bit."

"And you didn't handle the knife?"

"No, Officer Munday." I sat up straight and tried to appear law abiding and angelically innocent. I wondered if I could summon a halo.

"Ms. Turner, if you know more, it's best to tell us now. You are a person of interest in murder. That's a serious situation."

"Okay. Before he died, the man said 'diamond' and 'Dixie,' or at least that's what I thought he said. It made no sense. When I got up to leave, someone started yelling and suddenly, the manager was there with a baseball bat, and police were swarming the room."

"Yes, they were already in the hotel."

"When I talked to the manager the other day, he said that my so-called uncle and some woman had fought several times, even on the day of the murder. Have you found the woman who bumped into me at all or questioned the manager? He seems to be someone who creeps around the hotel a lot. He might have overheard something and killed my uncle, ah, the dead man himself. I would say he is as much a person of interest as I am. And the woman. She obviously had blood on her hands when she grabbed my arm."

"Are you lecturing us how to do our jobs, Ms. Turner?"

"No," I whispered, my head bowed.

He tapped his pen on the table. "I think I remember Chief Poe telling me about you."

I tilted my chin up in what I hoped was a chaste look.

"We *have* questioned him, and we *are* looking for the woman."

"She might be anywhere. She's a master of disguise," I said.

"How do you know that?"

"Well, I did some research. I'm a researcher, a genealogist. I looked up the words 'diamond' and 'Dixie' in several different ways. I came up with Diamond Dixies, a group of women who robbed jewelry stores in the 80s and 90s. I lost track of them, but they used a lot of tricks to disguise themselves. I think my mother was one of them, and I think this Mick Taylor and the other woman were involved. They might think my mother had money or diamonds hidden away somewhere."

"Whew, that's quite a story." He sat back in his chair with a puzzled look on his face.

"I mean, it does sound a bit like fiction, but with my mother, anything was possible. She might have actually been a thief," I said a bit too forcefully. Even though I had almost come to that unlikely conclusion, my words hung in the air like 500-pound turkeys laboring to fly.

"We'll look into it all," he said in way of appeasing me. He must have heard how unconvincing he sounded for he followed with, "Well, we might need copies of those articles if this turns out to be true. For the time being, just steer clear of the Grady Hotel and don't leave town." He nodded toward Charlotte. "Always a pleasure, Ms. Webb."

I went home and delved into my mother's boxes with a more intense eye, searching for any clues, margin scribbling, obscure notations, holding pages up to the light for invisible ink, but there was nothing. How many secrets had she taken to the grave?

Chapter 5

"Do you think your birth certificate is real?" Poe asked. He looked tired.

He was back from D.C., had listened to my condensed story over dinner, spent some time with Albie, and now was settled with his feet upon the hassock and a cup of Jenny's latest tea in his hand.

"I see you like my new footstool. I thought I would spruce up the apartment a bit. I'm also considering curtains."

"Trying to distract me with fancy décor ideas?"

"My décor is fancy?"

"No, just your footwork when you dance away from the issues in front of us." Poe gave me a serious look that worked into a smile. He saw me relax and added, "Listen, this is still a serious matter, and I don't like it when you get yourself involved. I don't know if it was your homemade cooking, Jenny's tea, or an exhausting day, but my anger has left the building. So, all I'll say for now is that I missed all this."

I wasn't sure what he meant by "all this," but I liked to think he was including me in the mix. "Okay. I doubt the birth certificate is real. I think my mother was trying to disappear, and she did a great job of it."

"How will you know for sure?"

"I guess I'll start at the office of Vital Records in California. Los Angeles and a hospital are listed. I can also check to see if it's a real hospital."

"Do you remember living in LA?"

"No, I don't." I suddenly snapped my fingers. "LA—Lala Land. I'm surprised she didn't write down Hollywood on the birth certificate. I wouldn't have put it past this woman to list that as the place I was born."

"With your skills, I know you will track it down." Poe took a sip of tea.

Doubts suddenly flooded my brain like a burst water pipe.

"What? You've remembered something?" Poe sat up.

"No, but what if my name isn't El Turner?" I started to feel sick. "What if I'm Lavinia Wildsmoott?" I started to panic. "I'm not sure I want to find out I'm a whole other person. It would be like some science fiction movie where a person walks through a wavy door and finds herself in another dimension. Some alternate world."

"Now, don't get ahead of yourself," Poe soothed. He put down his cup and reached for my hand, rubbing my palm with his thumb. "Didn't you counsel some woman last year who wanted to get married but had a ridiculous name? Didn't you tell her the person makes the name, not the other way around?"

"Okay, Mr. Smarty Pants. Thanks for the reminder, but I'm freaking out. I don't think I could handle that."

"We don't know anything at this point. Besides, you will always be El Turner." He got the devil in his eyes. "Of course, Lavinia does sound very fetching. I like it. I'm sure you could pull it off."

I grabbed a pillow and hit his arm. "This isn't funny."

"I know. Do you think your mother was wanted by

the law?" I almost choked on my tongue. I hadn't gotten into the Dixies with him yet, and I wasn't sure Detective Munday had brought it to his attention. I knew there were a lot of things on his plate to greet his return. I had planned to ease into this whole thing.

"My little old mother? What could she be guilty of?" I looked his way. "You haven't talked to Detective Munday?"

"I've been too busy catching up. You wouldn't believe how much paperwork goes with this job. What do you make of Uncle Mickey contacting you? There must be an angle somewhere, possibly a crime or crimes involved. He sure didn't seem on the level. And didn't you say you moved around a lot, even leaving places in the middle of the night?"

"Yes, quite often. Once I even had to leave my dog Magellan behind."

"Magellan?"

I shrugged. "He was my favorite explorer at the time. I was home schooled. Which means my mother often just piled a bunch of schoolbooks on my desk and left me to figure things out."

I suddenly sat up. A vivid scene popped into my head. I wasn't prepared for all these surges of memory.

"What?" Poe asked concerned.

"Ever since I started this backtracking of my life, little flashback slivers have jumped out of hiding and tried to scare me. They're doing a pretty good job of it."

"What did you remember? Something about the dog?"

"Yes. When I first saw it. I remember waking up hearing a dog bark. I went into the kitchen in my pajamas, and there was a puppy. The man holding him said something that sounded like 'good cover.' I thought that was the dog's name and cried, 'Here, Cover. Come here, Cover.' The man thought it was hilarious and didn't stop laughing. Looking back, I wonder if he was saying that having a dog would be a good cover story for her."

"What did your mother say?"

"She immediately said I could name the dog anything I wanted and shooed the man out of the house. Not many people came to our house, and when they did, it was late at night."

"Do you remember the man at all? Could it have been Uncle Mickey?"

"To tell you the truth, all I had eyes for was the dog. Speaking of which, Uncle Mickey did say he remembered my serious blue eyes. I was too shocked to ask him about it in the park, but he must have been around when I was little. Am I crazy?"

"We've confirmed that your uncle's name was Mick Taylor. Just appeared in 1980. No record of him before. It's probably a fake name, and one that is very common."

"With my mother's crowd, I'm not surprised. Did you find an address for him? Anything to track him, like fingerprints?"

"Not so far. Believe it or not, his fingerprints were mutilated."

"What does that mean?

"Somewhere along the line he used acid or scraped them. A method to avoid detection was used, and we have to figure out who he is. We aren't some big government agency, so our methods are a bit slower."

"Wow. I've never heard of that."

"You'd be surprised. People use all kinds of ways to avoid being identified."

"You may not know him, but can you put my mother's name in your crime database and check? I know it's not real, but there might be something. A hint. A clue."

"El, I can't use it for personal means.

"But she might have been the sister of the victim. Maybe he was telling the truth about that." I tried the legal angle. "If you find out something about her, you might be able to identify him."

"You're right. And we've got nothing on him yet to prove any connection. If he was involved in theft or fencing, he must have been good. Stayed in the shadows. Name leads nowhere."

"Well, he couldn't have been too successful. He was staying at the Grady, and his clothes smelled like mothballs."

"I noticed that. We are testing for drugs. That might have been his downfall."

"Do you really think he and my mother could have been bank robbers or jewel thieves?" I tried to sound excited.

"Okay, El. I know you too well. What secrets are you holding onto that I need to know?"

"Well, I wasn't sure what they were, and I didn't want to burden you."

"Well, now's the time to burden me."

"Uncle Mickey said something before he died. I had no idea what he meant or even if I heard him correctly."

"And you didn't tell the officer because you wanted to investigate more?"

"I did tell him," I proclaimed, trying to look as innocent as a ghost in a churchyard. "I wanted to run it by you as well."

"So, what did Uncle Mick say?"

"He said what sounded like 'diamond' and 'Dixie.'"

Albie shuffled over to the cage door and squawked, "145 664 823 144."

"Albie, you have to quit doing that!" I shouted, jumping up and pulling my hand from Poe's. I put one hand over my thumping heart and shook a finger at the bird with the other. My nerves were anything but relaxed.

"Ah, the numbers! I wondered if we would hear them again. Did you get them this time?" Poe's mind went to more practical matters. He stood up and moved toward the cage.

"It was so quick; I didn't get it. All my writing materials are now in the other bedroom instead of handy on the kitchen table." I glanced over to the uncluttered table, now gracing a jar of flowers. "What set him off?"

"What were we talking about before he squawked numbers?"

"Just that Uncle Mickey had said something that sounded like 'diamond' and 'Dixie.'"

Albie squawked again. "145 664 823 144."

"Diamond and Dixie," Poe repeated.

Again, the numbers echoed around the room. Albie seemed to be dancing around his cage, something he did when he was expecting a treat.

"Okay. I think we have the key to unlock them. Get a pen and paper."

I was ready when Poe said, "Diamond and Dixie."

"I got them." I handed the paper to Poe. "Do they mean anything to you?"

"Twelve numbers. Not a thing. Not a phone number. Maybe a bank account?"

"A bank account!" I shouted. "Do you think my mother had some money or diamonds stashed?"

Albie screeched out the numbers again.

"Okay. Let's not mention d-i-a-m-o-n-d-s again." Poe spelled out the word. "How about we stick to jewels or jewelry or loot?" He raised his voice. We heard the sound of loud vacuuming just outside my door in the hall.

"Time to spill my secrets," I said. "I did some research, and I think my mother was a jewel thief, you-know-what kind mostly. I came across a gang of two, maybe three women, using a variety of disguises, and I'm almost positive my mother was one. It seems like the woman in Uncle Mickey's room was probably another. They hit a lot of jewelry stores over several decades. There might have been more, but a lot were not reported in the newspapers. If Uncle Mickey and that woman were after some jewels, I don't know where they would be." The room got quiet again as the vacuuming stopped.

"I sent the sketch you left out to other police stations. They will be looking for her. I have a hunch that she didn't go far. I think she's still around. And if the gang was good at disguise, she could be anywhere."

"Wow. To think one's mother or pseudo-mother could be a jewel thief."

"And you didn't find any references to anything in those boxes?" Poe pointed to the extra room where I had stowed my mother's things.

"Not much. A stack of old receipts. A few old magazines she had been reading before she died. Clothes. No legal documents. If there were any and Mason Street, her old lawyer, had them, who knows where they are since he's long gone. She didn't keep much."

"So why would she keep old receipts?"

"Good question. Let me get them."

I dug around, found them and a pair of high-heeled shoes, and brought them back to Poe.

"What's with the shoes?" he asked.

"I've read where people hide things in the heels of shoes." I got a screwdriver and pried one heel loose from the shoe, then the other. Nothing. I shrugged. "Worth a try. I'm not sure why she kept them. She always wore flat house slippers."

"Looks like she blacked out most of the information. Can't even see what they were for." Poe was examining the receipts.

"Why would she black out the name of the place?" I asked. "Very suspicious." I was hoping he might spot something I had missed.

Poe flicked through them all. "Must have been important and one she didn't want anyone to find."

I was getting excited. "This is like a treasure hunt."

Poe glanced up at me. "A deadly one. Remember one man has died possibly because of this. Best to keep this quiet." He put his finger to his lips, got up from the sofa, and walked quietly to the door. He pulled it open.

An older woman in a uniform was bent over a vacuum cleaner very close to my door. She looked up with a surprised expression on her face. She stood and moved on down the hall. Poe waited in the open doorway until we heard the machine start up again.

When he came back, he was the grim policeman. "Lock your doors well, and be careful," he repeated. "Don't open this door to anyone you don't know."

"Aren't you getting a bit anxious over some woman

vacuuming the hall?"

"No. It's my job to be suspicious. Didn't you say the women could disguise themselves in many ways? I'm being extra cautious here. I'm sure you don't know the word, but it means—"

"Yeah. Yeah. I get it."

"I'm jetlagged. I better stumble home while I can. Tomorrow will be another long day." He gathered his hat.

I said good night, double locked the doors, put a chair under the knob, and went to bed. I woke up several times with nightmares I couldn't remember, but I heard nothing unusual. In the end, I got up before the sun, made coffee, and searched France for Hannah B's aunt.

****

I spent the morning in France, and then decided I needed a break. The world reigned smoky with chaos. Too much confusion in my life made me cranky and unfocused. I needed to get back to some sort of reality, some way to anchor my feet to the ground of common sense and away from the eye of the police. I wondered if Jenny would agree to take a nice long drive with me. Getting in a car, the windows open, the radio turned up, had always felt like freedom to me.

When I knocked on her door, however, there was no answer. In one sense, I was delighted. I felt like I was about to play hooky from school. In another sense, I felt the guilt of not letting Jenny know where I was. I'd put a note on her door to at least show the attempt to let her know. There was also the fear which seemed to hide in all the dim corners. It made me jumpy.

I was hyper cautious, edging my way down the stairs, constantly darting my head around to see in every direction. It wasn't until I was safely in the car and heading out of the garage that I knew where to go. It might have been in the back of my mind all along. If there had ever been anyone more normal and down to earth, it was Susie Q Hawkins.

When Rita's friend Timmy had been killed last year, I had done some investigating, one of which was a trip to explore the alley where he had been murdered. Seeing two people at a house nearby, I decided to ask them if they had seen anything on that night. The two people turned out to be Susie Q and Hubie Hawkins, an elderly couple who had opened an ache in my heart for what it must be like to have grandparents. Susie Q had been full of southern hospitality with her gentle ways and heavily sugared sweet tea. Hubie had been just the opposite, loud and opinionated, but one could see how much he cared for and listened to Susie Q. At the time, I had wanted to visit with them again and again, just to pretend they were my grandparents. And right now, I badly needed a dose of down to earth.

I had to backtrack several streets to find the one on which they lived. I remembered the area had been in a bit of development when I had met them, new age stores that Hubie had ranted against. It seemed most of the people along their street had been selling out to the developer. Hubie let the whole neighborhood know, loudly and frankly, that he was not one of them.

The bright lights everywhere were the first thing that baffled me. It seemed like every business along there had neon flashings of some kind. The stores were all in a row and looked like the strip malls of the 1950s and 60s in structure. Maybe they were cool and retro at this point. Gone were the remaining trees and greenery. I drove along the street, trying to find the Hawkins home among the stores. I didn't see it. I drove back and forth several times, but it was not there. Even the alley where Timmy had been murdered was bricked over and painted with a giant sunflower.

I parked my car and decided to go into one of the stores and ask if they knew what happened to the Hawkins family. Parking was busy for early afternoon, but I found a spot in front of the Rusty Lantern. Despite the old-fashioned name, there wasn't a lantern in sight. Fancy table lamps, decorative stands with metallic shades, futuristic hanging globes, and chandeliers of unimaginable creation glittered and blazed like the world was on fire. The young girl in charge had no idea what happened to the people who had had houses there and didn't really care. When she found out I didn't need a $300 lamp, she lost interest.

I thought the next business, Coin-o-rama, was possibly a laundry, but it turned out to be an arcade. The windows had been spray painted so it was hard to tell. The noise inside was deafening. Children screamed and laughed and shouted, and I left as quickly as possible.

I had no idea what the Gilded Lily was selling since their windows featured large dining tables with immaculate place settings and seated mannequins dressed like it was the Roaring Twenties. One window displayed the words *Vintage Vogue*; the other proclaimed *Affordable Luxury*. The oxymorons outweighed the urge to enter, and I moved on.

Then I saw what I took to be an ice cream shop. It was called 47 ½ flavors. I was shocked when it turned out to be exactly that, a place that sold ice cream. It was also wildly popular, but there were several older people who looked like they might know what happened to the families who had lived there. After making my way to a few tables, I got the idea they were mostly there for the ice cream and knew nothing about what had come before. They were shocked to find out there had been a before.

My afternoon of freedom and disappointment seemed to scream for a treat, so I got in line. As I moved closer to the glass cases, I saw two young men rushing around like rivers in a storm filling orders. The monitors behind them flashed pictures of ice cream with strange names, but looking at the constant motion gave me a headache. I tried to read the names on some of the ice cream containers, but the line was full of kids who insisted on being front and center with their noses pressed to the glass. They made it impossible to peek over their excited heads.

I happened to look at the wall below the monitors and saw a yellowed newspaper clipping with a picture of what looked like Susie Q and Hubie. Strain as I could, I was not able to make out the particulars. When it was my turn, I asked the young man with the spiky red hair, harried attitude, and crisp white hat if he knew who the people in the article were. I pointed toward the wall. He shook his head, not understanding, not even turning around.

"Who are the people in that article?" I raised my voice louder.

"What kind did you say?"

I tried a different tactic. "I wanted to know about that clipping on the wall. Can I come back there and look at it?"

He appeared horrified. "No one is allowed back here

but qualified personnel." I wondered how qualified one had to be to scoop ice cream.

"Can you take it off the wall so I can look at it?"

"Ma'am, you are holding up the line. What kind of ice cream did you want?" Now he was agitated. I had gotten him out of his rhythm of ask, scoop, serve.

I looked behind me and the line had grown out the door. I still didn't know what they had. I remembered their sign. "I'll take the half flavor."

"The what?"

"You advertise forty-seven and a half flavors. I'd like to try the half."

"Are you looking for trouble, lady?" he whispered out of the side of his mouth.

"Not at all. I want to try the half, please."

"What kind?" he sighed, rolling his eyes at the woman behind me.

"What do you mean what kind? Don't you have forty-seven and a half different flavors?"

"Yes, but you can have whatever flavor you want."

I had had enough, and so had he. "Strawberry, please." Now I just wanted to move the line along.

"Do you want Hunka Hunka Strawberry, Ghost Chile Strawberry, Strawberry Mushroom Surprise…?"

I stopped him right there. "Just give me the plainest strawberry flavor you have."

He took out a small scoop and a cup and placed a smidgen of a dollop of ice cream in it. "This variety is called For the Mild Adventurer Strawberry. That will be ten-fifty. Pay over there." He pointed to a girl seated near the register.

"Did you say ten-fifty? For that little scoop of ice cream?" I could hear the murmurs behind me growing louder with calls to "move it along."

"Lady, you said you wanted the half scoop flavor. That's it. You wanted the plain strawberry, that's it."

"But why does it cost so much?" I could hear children crying behind me, whining to their parents that they wanted ice cream.

"The extra charge is for the half scoop." He pushed my cupped dot of ice cream down the counter toward the register. He was more than ready to be done with me.

"But it's not even the size of the regular scoop."

"You pay extra for the fun of getting half a scoop."

"Fun?" I had come this way looking for common sense but felt like I had stepped into a bizarro world of absurdity.

"Look, lady, you want to be a troublemaker, do it somewhere else. We have people who want to be served."

"Well, I changed my mind." I stood my ground. "I'm not in the mood for that much fun." I headed for the door. People cheered my leaving.

As the clapping subsided, I heard the world "police" as I opened the door.

I ran to my car not wanting a police escort to the station. Just as I fit the key into the ignition, a realization hit me like a scoop of 47 and ½ flavors. I did so much research in old newspapers and those from around the country, I didn't pay much attention to the local ones. All I had to do was search the local papers for the article that had been on the wall. It must have come from the Parkville paper. I would prevail over insanity.

****

The article was as disappointing as the line of modern stores had been.

The picture was of Susie Q and Hubie Hawkins, but the clipping was not one I wanted to read. Being the last house standing in the way of the developer's dream of a "re-imagined" strip mall, the Hawkins family home had sold for a record amount of money. "Can't stand in the way of progress," Hubie had been quoted as saying. At least Susie Q appeared to have a tear in her eye as she was handed the check.

Asked about plans for all that money, Hubie replied that they were moving to Maui where he was going to open a surfboard business, a dream he had long held. The other half of the business would be Susie Q's Sweet Tea Shop. "I believe in sticking to my roots," she had said.

I decided to write ice cream off my food list forever.

Chapter 6

"Well, that certainly sounded like an interesting conversation," Poe said as I got off the phone. Now that he was back, he had taken to coming over in the evening. Often, he brought groceries, and I did the cooking, or takeout like tonight. I had come a long way from my history of canned soup.

"You aren't going to believe this. That was the man who was living with my mother before she died."

"Wasn't he a poet or something?" Poe set the table. "Do my eyes deceive me? Have you invested in some matching dishes while I was gone? Or did we borrow from Jenny again?"

I ignored his dig and continued. "Yes, a Mr. Taylor. I think it was Samuel Taylor. Wait! You don't think he's related to my dear old Uncle Mickey, do you? Maybe they are all related. A gang of Taylors. Maybe they used the same fake name. Do you think he was in on this as well?"

"I can check him out. Did he say where he was staying?"

"No. And I don't care if he was a poet or not; he ran when the going got tough. Even if she wasn't my mother, I couldn't run out on her."

"What did he want?" Poe began to unpack the takeout food.

"He wants Albie back." I sat down at the table and

loaded my plate.

"What? After all this time?" Poe looked and sounded puzzled. "Did he say why?"

"No. When I told him the bird had been abandoned at the pet store by my mother, he offered to buy him. Gave me a huge figure too."

"That's strange. I'll check out the name. If there is some connection, we'll find it, but I don't have my hopes up. It seems like there are a lot of phony names floating around."

"What's also strange is that Josh, you remember that guy from the pet store, also called me last week asking to buy him. Said he got attached when Albie was at his store so long."

"Okay. Something's going on. Those numbers Albie spouted must mean something important. Maybe you can do some research into them. There might be international connections. Please wait for me to go with you to the pet store. We can ask Josh questions together."

"But why now?"

"Because of your mother's death, I would imagine, or Uncle Mickey's death. Did you run an obituary in the newspaper with her name?"

"I did. Do you think that's what opened the door to all this?"

"If they were looking for your mother, they might have been keeping tabs on that name. An obituary would be a giant red flag. Something's definitely in play."

"Have you come up with any other suspects for his murder beside me?"

"We're looking into the case," he said, but I knew enough not to push.

"Will you let me know before you come to arrest

me?" I tried to play it lightly. Being the chief person of interest was not a happy place. "I hope you remember I thought the manager might have done it. Also, my mother's supposed crime partner. And I wouldn't bypass Mr. Poet either." I ticked off the list on my fingers. "Then there's Mr. X."

"Mr. X?" Poe stopped eating and gave me a quizzical look.

"The unknown. The person in the shadows. The one we haven't discovered yet."

"Oh, him."

"Or her."

"Oh, him or her. That person."

"It's not funny. I can't be the major star in this drama."

"Maybe we should get Rita back here to play the role," Poe said. "No, wait. On second thought, that wouldn't work. You two might double the trouble." He smiled then changed the subject. "By the way, I came up in the elevator with Jenny and what looked like her new beau."

"Beau? Is that still a word?" I teased.

"Call me old fashioned, many do, but they sure looked chummy."

"What's he like?" I imagined a gray-haired yoga guru or some tie-dyed beatnik carrying a bongo under his arm.

"She introduced him as Mr. Sweetie."

"Mr. Sweetie? That's his name?"

"That's what it sounded like. She was mumbling. She turned all shades of red too." Poe laughed. "Actually, the guy was wearing a sharp blue suit, clean white shirt, and silk tie. Crew cut brown hair. No facial fuzz. Almost the exact opposite, wouldn't you say?"

"Wow! Well, whoever he is, I'm glad she has company. Was she taking him to her apartment?"

"She had a look like I was going to arrest her for having a man in her room or something." He snapped his fingers. "Maybe he was a male escort."

"Okay, now you're stretching things. What's gotten into you tonight? You sure are spunky." My voice was rising above the noise outside.

"Spunky? Is that still a word?"

"Touché. Let's talk about something else."

Again, we could hear vacuuming out in the hallway, close to my door and very loud. Then it stopped.

"What's with all the noise in the evening? Isn't it late for cleaning? I have my suspicions about that woman." Poe put his finger to his lips and got up from the table.

"Yes, Mr. McGaffey always cleans during the day," I whispered. "Maybe he quit."

I went to the door and opened it, Poe right behind me. The vacuum went back on. A woman in kerchief and apron was working her way down the hall. I had the feeling she had been listening at our door.

"Hello!" I called. "Where's Mr. McGaffey?"

"*No hablo ingles*," she shouted over the vacuum.

"*Yo hablo Espanol*." Mr. Marquez's Spanish lessons were finally paying off.

She changed her speech. "He's sick. I sub." She didn't turn around but kept the machine going.

I closed the door and went back to the table. "Working late to catch up, I guess. I had the feeling she was listening in at the door."

"I don't like it," Poe said. "I had that same feeling

the other night when she was out there. Remember all those chains and bolts you had put in last year? Use them, please."

"Because of a cleaning lady?" I tried to smile.

"That and the calls. Didn't you say your mother's gang was into disguises? Take it seriously."

"But some woman who's vacuuming hallways?"

"Like I said, I'm just naturally suspicious. And didn't you tell me they could dress up as anyone, old or young? There's something odd there. I'm not sure, but maybe we should put Albie into witness protection."

"Protection!" Albie and I cried together.

"Let's just be cautious. Do any of those newspaper clippings talk about the last job those women pulled? Do they say where the robberies took place and exactly what was taken?"

I had sorted them by date and had made a makeshift map of places. "This was the last mention I could find, but I think that was so long ago, it doesn't count. I have no idea when their last job was or what it was or even where it was. I only know that my mother came to Parkville, but she could have been hiding out somewhere else. I could check large robberies on a global scale. See if anything there refers to jewels."

"How long was your mother in Parkville before you came?"

"Easy enough to find out." I started making a list.

"I hate to speculate, but what if your mother kept the spoils from the last job, and the other woman or women were cut out? That might have meant a lot of lost money for Uncle Mickey as well. Maybe your mother left them before the split. Maybe she left with Mr. Poet and came to Parkville. Maybe Mr. Poet didn't know the full range of her activities, but he had an inkling. Caught her teaching Albie the numbers or something. It might not be possible to trace your mom's movements, but it might be easier to check the poet's history. That is, if he didn't change his name too. Who knows where they met."

"I can try to trace him and see what I can find. I do remember when I came to Parkville, my mother would often repeat things over and over when she thought I wasn't listening. Her mind was still sharp, even at the end, so I didn't understand. We know she was cagey and put out a lot of breadcrumbs. She could lay traps of misleading clues. She never wanted to write things down. She might have been repeating words just to lead me off the trail. What trail, I don't know. I could imagine her teaching something to a bird as a decoy. But why? Was it just a distraction? And where would she put the money or whatever she kept, and what could the numbers mean? Or maybe the numbers are meaningless. There was no key anywhere for a safety deposit box. She might have just set up a host of false quests. It's so hard to know. Why couldn't she have been just a normal mother?" I groaned. "You don't know how lucky you are to be part of a regular family."

"All families have issues." Poe shrugged. "There's too much interest in your mother for this all to be a hoax. Somewhere your mother stashed something of value. Do you still have those receipts you found?"

When I brought them back, he said, "These might have some relation as to where whatever she was hiding could be. Possibly they are receipts for a yearly rental of a safe deposit box or something. But she would need a key for that, and you haven't found one. She'd be sure to keep them to show proof. Did she have a bank account where the money could be? Maybe she converted whatever she had into cash."

"I don't know. Her old lawyer Mason Street, the one who skipped town, never mentioned a bank account. If she did have one, he might not have known. Maybe he emptied out her account or found whatever treasure she had hid."

"If you remember, and I think you still do, he left in a hurry. Not sure he had time to clean out any account or go hunting for treasure."

I sighed. "Let's not go down that memory lane. I'll contact local banks and check. And, yes, she was just devious enough to leave worthless clues behind." I added banks to the list. "If she did sell off the goods, wouldn't that be a lot of money? Can you find out if there is anything in the police files for Mason Street? What happened to the files he left behind when he left town in such a hurry? There might have been a file on my mother."

"I'll do what I can. For now, my brain is thoroughly confused. With a motherly influence like that, how did you end up as sweet and wholesome as you are?" He got up and went into the kitchen for more coffee.

I liked the idea he thought I was sweet. Where along the line had I acquired sweetness?

Poe laughed as he came back into the room. "Now can we switch mysteries to the one about Jenny and her new man?"

****

"So do you miss me?"

"Rita! Yes! Yes! It's so good to hear your voice," I cried over the phone the next morning, glad to hear from my ex-neighbor and mystery partner-in-crime.

"How's old Parkville doing without its society director?" Rita referred to her old column in the local newspaper.

"Not the same at all. We all miss your gossip column."

"It was a society column." She huffed.

As much as she had bothered me with her constant visits when she lived down the hall, I felt an ache in my heart hearing her voice. "I miss you. No one comes and paces around my kitchen anymore."

"Well, I miss you too." She laughed into the phone. "What's up with you? Any new family trees to sniff around?"

"Now that's funny." My chuckle came out a bit late. I could hear her mind at work.

"Now what aren't you telling me? You know I certainly can sniff out a story, even over the phone, and I don't need a family tree to do it."

I hesitated before answering. "Well, in fact, I've become a person of interest."

"A person of interest for what?"

"How quickly you forget."

"OMG, El! The police think you murdered someone?"

"Yes, they do."

"Are you fooling with me? Is this a joke? You know it's not funny."

"No joke. I promise."

"So, who did you supposedly murder? And have you talked to the press yet?" I could see her taking out her pen and notebook.

"You remember that whole deal with my mother? Well, this man came around claiming to be my uncle and that he had information for me. When I went to his hotel room, I found him dead, and people discovered me over the dead body."

"Shot?"

"You won't believe this."

"Not a knife. That would be too freaky."

"Freaky it may be, but that's the truth."

"Who was he? What information did he have? Where was he from?"

"I'm not telling you this to find it in some New York paper with your byline."

I heard a loud sigh. "Okay. But give me the exclusive when you do. The first murder case in little old Parkville was what got me to the big city and those juicy bylines."

I hesitated again, debating how much to tell her, but erred on the side of caution.

"The police are investigating. Not much so far. I'll keep you informed, don't worry." I changed the subject. "How's Reb these days? Is there a wedding date yet?"

"Actually, Reb got transferred to New Orleans. He was so serious. He really changed after he came here. He was worried about me all the time. Made me take all sorts of defense classes because I was often out late following stories. Hand-to-hand combat, martial arts, you name it. He really drilled me on that. Even took me to the gun range on weekends and taught me to shoot. I hated to say goodbye to him, but it was for the best. He was getting a tad bit jealous, and this city is full of hunky men."

I had to question her statement. From what I remembered, Reb Wilson got more than just a tad bit jealous. Even in Parkville, he was intense, following Rita around when she wasn't aware. When Rita had disappeared last year to protect herself, I had suspected Reb of doing away with her. He had some strange undertones.

But Rita was not to be shaken off so easily. "If you need me to come back and help you out of your jam, I'm ready. Just remember that. I can be there at the drop of a Chief of Police's hat."

"Good one. Thanks, but Jenny got me a lawyer, so I'm all set."

"But what about finding out who really did it? Who's going to help there? Are there suspects?"

"This time I'm leaving it in the hands of the police."

"Okay. What have you done with the real El Turner?"

"I guess I've changed."

"Not on your life. I bet you have researched each person involved and a few more besides. I know you. You can't let it go."

I laughed. She knew me too well. "Really, Rita. Poe has it in hand."

"And how is the mighty inspector? Still coming over to visit Albie?" I felt like she was in the room with me. How easy it was to think back on all the time she spent in this apartment.

"He's fine. Busy."

"I think I really might have to come back just to see for myself what's going on."

I tried to get her off the subject. "By the way, someone new has moved into your apartment."

"It's about time. How long were they going to let that sit?"

"I think they regarded it as a shrine. You know, to honor Parkville's redheaded journalist hero."

"Ha! Well, I certainly hope it's a good-looking man. Poe needs some competition."

"It's not a man. Remember Ida Parks from the library? It's her cousin. I think Ida said she was a standup comedian or something. I just met her for a few minutes before she left for her gigs, as she called them. She has a pair of cacti she wants me to look in on. Make sure they are behaving themselves."

"Funny. She didn't give you her key, did she?"

"As a matter of fact, she did."

"With all that has happened, don't be trading keys with anyone. You never know who will come storming into your apartment when you don't want them to."

"Yes. I certainly wouldn't want that to happen," I said.

She realized what she had said, and the laughter began again. "I hope she doesn't become famous. There is room for only one star to emerge from that apartment."

We chatted for a bit longer, catching up, more laughs, surface talk, but she was right. No matter what, I couldn't let the whole business go.

****

I contacted the manager of the house my mother had rented when she moved to Parkville. She had always paid in cash, he said, but he had a bit of time to talk to me. I drove over to see him, telling Jenny where I was going, and carrying my can of pepper spray. I knew I should have let Poe know where I was going too, but it seemed a harmless enough excursion. I looked around just to be sure and didn't spot a tail, either police or enemy. Would I be doing this for the rest of my life?

The manager was a squat, round fellow with fluffy gray hair. When I showed him the proof of relationship from Mason Street, he let me look at my mother's application. It was all lies, but I asked for a copy anyway. When I showed him the blacked-out receipts, he shook his head, eager to get on to other business.

I took the original death certificate, one of the blacked-out receipts, and a handful of IDs to the next item on my list: the banks. My first visit was to the bank my mother had used. Records showed an account with minimal use and a balance that wouldn't point to any diamond money. The receipt meant nothing to them.

The next four bank tellers I spoke to had no idea what I was showing them. The receipts were not theirs. At the next stop, I noticed the woman. I had seen her at one of the other banks: blonde, wide brimmed hat, large glasses, scarf around her neck, smart suit. It seemed too much of a coincidence.

In the interest of caution and confusion, I decided to double back to the first bank. This time, I asked for the manager and inquired about their safety deposit boxes. I thanked him and moved on. I checked the bank on leaving but did not see the blonde hair or the hat. Then I saw her in one of the cars in the parking lot. She had taken the hat off, but the blonde hair was unmistakable. I pretended to talk on my phone but tried to take a picture while doing so. I wasn't sure if it would show anything or not. I hoped it wouldn't show my thumb or the asphalt. I was still a newbie at this cloak and dagger stuff.

I then drove back to the second bank and asked to open a safety deposit box. The clerk led me into the vault, showed me the layout, but I said I would think about it. I repeated the process at each of the other banks. If the clerks noticed my return, no one said anything. At the last bank, I was taken into the vault. While shoving my keys into my pocket, I accidentally dropped one of the receipts. When the woman bent to retrieve it, I decided it wouldn't hurt to ask if it had come from her bank.

"Not from this bank; however, my boyfriend had his stuff in storage for a while. That looks like the same kind of receipt."

"Do you know the name of the place?"

"No. It was several years ago. We went there once, and I remember the buildings were all gray sheds in a row. Don't know if that helps."

She had just described what every storage company in the world looked like. But I continued my search through all the banks just the same and kept my side vision handy. I thought I spotted the mysterious woman several times, but my imagination was running at full speed. Could this be the woman who had bumped into me in the hallway of the Grady on the night of my uncle's murder? What did she think I had? Could she have been the killer?

I decided to call Poe to update him. He was busy, so I just went home.

The message light was blinking on my phone. I pressed play.

"Hi, Ms. Turner. This is Josh from the Ravin' Pet Store again. I have really missed old Albie and wondered if you changed your mind about selling him. I really do love that bird. Call me back."

Poe was right. Something was stirring, and I did not like it one little bit.

****

Email to Hannah B.
Dear Hannah—
Thank you for sending a copy of her birth certificate,

her high school diploma, and the photos. I'm afraid the death certificate you found for Wilhelmina Stone does not belong to your aunt. Wilhelmina had a family of record that is not yours. I'm curious about your aunt's religious aspect. What religion is your family? (If you don't mind saying.)
Best,
El Turner

****

Email to El Turner
Sorry to get that news, but it was a long shot. Our family is Catholic. Does that have significance? My younger sister seems to think she might have gone to California.
Thanks,
Hannah

Chapter 7

I tried Poe off and on throughout the afternoon, but all I got was a terse, "I'll have to call you back." I couldn't wait to tell him what I found out about the receipt. Tomorrow I would hit the storage companies to see if the receipts matched. I'd make a list of the businesses so we could be ready. I thought I would wait before I told him more about the woman who seemed to be following me. Was it the woman who had run into me at the Grady? I shoved my paranoia back into its hole and charged forward. The city was small, and it wasn't unusual to run into the same person twice.

Poe did not knock on my door that night. I ate a lonely dinner and talked to Albie until he nestled into his wing.

The next morning, I decided to walk to Mr. Marquez's store for a newspaper before going to the market.

"*Buenos dias, Senor Marquez.* First off, *Felicidades!* I heard you had been appointed to the Board of the Parkville Historical Society."

"*Gracias, El. En verdad es un honor.*"

"Yes, it is indeed an honor."

"Miss Cassie as well was appointed," he said.

"I heard that! *De nuevo, Felicidades!*" El said. "Someone also mentioned that you are donating the prints you had in the store here to the Parkville Historical

Society. I remember how much people loved seeing them when they were on display at the library."

"Yes. If I donate them, more people will have the chance to view them. It is a matter of pride for our family."

"As it should be. They are a lovely collection, and I'm sure the Historical Society will treat them with care."

He bowed his head and then gave me a grin. "*Que año.*"

"Yes, quite a year! I finally had a chance to use my Spanish yesterday," I said.

"That's good, El, but it would be better if I heard that in Spanish."

"*Lo siento. Me disculpo,*" I stumbled through.

"*Gracias.*"

"I'm sure I will mangle this, but I think you employ the same cleaning service. Mr. McGaffey, one of our building's cleaning crew, did not show up the other day. His sub was a woman who said she spoke no English, so I told her I spoke Spanish. She then switched to an abbreviated English. Now that I think about it, I wonder if she even knew Spanish or just pretended. Anyway, I wonder if you have talked to Mr. McGaffey lately."

"No, but his nephew cleans our store in the evening, and he told us Mr. McGaffey received a very large bonus from an employer and decided to take a long vacation."

"That's odd. The woman said he had called in sick."

"We should all be that kind of sick. His nephew said he was going to spend his time fishing and swimming. He rented a cottage near some big lake."

I got the newspaper, but outside storm clouds were forming. Would I have to be suspicious of all women from now on? The cleaning woman? The woman waiting at the corner bus stop? The woman traffic cop cruising by my apartment? I hurried on to the market. The curious was getting curiouser and curiouser.

****

When I returned from the market with a full cart, I saw my building was surrounded by police cars. Poe stood outside near one of the cruisers.

"El, where have you been? I've been trying to call you."

"Sorry, I guess I turned my phone off. What's going on?"

"Let's go inside."

As we entered the lobby, I saw Albie in his cage taking treats from Albert, the door manager.

"What in the world is Albie doing here?"

"It looks like someone broke into your apartment and tried to make off with Albie."

I was stunned. "Make off with Albie?"

"Luckily Albert here didn't buy the person's story."

"I'm so sorry! He must have slipped in when I was helping old Mrs. Worth with her packages. When I spotted the young man with Albie, I confronted him. He said he was taking him out for a spa day. Have his feathers washed and clipped. When I questioned him and asked for ID, he ran out the door with Albie. He was wearing a hooded sweatshirt and sunglasses, so I couldn't see his face. I was so shocked; I didn't notice how tall he was. He was a fast runner though. Well, I chased right after him. Albie was squawking all the way. Screaming *Murder*! *Murder*! Just like when you were kidnapped."

"Yes, I remember that well," I interrupted.

"Well, everyone on the street was looking, so he put

Albie down on the sidewalk and took off down an alley. We tried to catch him, but he was too quick for us. I doubled back and retrieved the bird."

"Albert, you're a hero. Thank you!"

"That bird sure makes a racket when he wants to, doesn't he?" Albert shook his head.

"Yes, he sure does."

"Looks like the guy broke into your apartment. Guess we will have to get you another lock. Time to call the locksmith again. Maybe you should put him on speed dial?" Poe's face gave off the very definition of grim.

"I'm sorry, Miss Turner, but the management will not view this in a good light," Albert said. "I will have to submit a report. They like to advertise this as a safe and quiet environment."

"It's not her fault," Poe said.

"Of course not, sir. I didn't mean to imply anything at all. I just do have a responsibility to the management to keep everyone here safe."

"If the management has any questions, please refer them to me," Poe said, giving Albert his card. Poe took charge of Albie.

I went up to the apartment with Poe to find an officer guarding my door. A crowbar leaned against the wall.

"Why does this keep happening to me?" I groaned. "I just want to live a normal, quiet life. Now I sound like a broken record."

"Do you see anything else taken?" Poe asked. He put Albie back in his usual spot. He tried to rub the side of Albie's head, but Albie was having none of it. He edged back and forth along his perch, bobbing his head vigorously.

"Nothing disturbed. My pile of clippings and

research is still on the desk." I would have to put them away, out of sight.

"Seriously, El, maybe you and Albie should go somewhere for a while. I'll leave an officer here until the lock gets fixed." He left the apartment, mind already onto something else demanding his attention.

He was gone before I realized I had not told him my discovery.

****

The new locksmith came right away. Poe also installed a police car on the street which limited my outside access. I suppose I could have snuck out the back way, but what if someone was waiting there? I didn't want to chance it. It stopped me from checking out the storage companies. Truth was, I was scared. Someone was not afraid to break down my door (which caused a lot of noise), steal a bird, and try to get away. Where was he going? Was there a getaway car? It didn't help matters that Albie shouted *Murder! Murder!* every time I left the room or was out of eyesight. Treats would not soothe him.

From Albert's description, the person who broke down my door could have been anyone. Was it the manager of the hotel? The poet Taylor? Josh from Ravin' Pet Store? The last two had been awfully anxious to get Albie in their clutches. When I got a chance, I was going to go down to the shop and talk to Josh. But for now, I could call.

"Ravin' Pet Store, Linda speaking."

"Josh, please."

"Oh, he's not in today. He called in sick. Guess he has the flu or something. Can I take a message, or can I help you with something?"

"Thanks, but I'll call back."

Out sick. It could have been him. I called the hotel.

"May I speak to the manager, please?"

"I'm sorry. He's out today. Can I take a message?"

"Thanks, I'll call back."

Two suspects were not where they were supposed to be. Who was to say it was a man. It could have been the women who knocked into me at the hotel and was possibly following me around town. She was good at disguises. But she was older. Could she run that quickly? I wasn't sure how many women were in my mother's gang. Maybe there were two women floating around keeping watch on me. And what about the poet? I didn't know where he was staying, but I had his number. When I called back, I just got a voicemail.

I went into the kitchen for another coffee.

"Murder! Murder!" Albie shouted hysterically.

"I'm right here, Albie. It's okay. Somebody wants those numbers you know. I wish you could tell me what they were for."

If I was stuck inside, I would research. That always calmed me down. Real life was much too frantic to consider at present. Where to start? With a direction away from me and my problems, I'd see what I could find out regarding Hannah B's aunt. Searching took an hour, but I soon hit the jackpot. Wilma Stone had joined a convent in California. Luckily this was an order that reported given names on census forms as well as those taken in the convent. Sister Mary Catherine, aka Wilma Stone. I sent requests to the archivist of the order as well as to the Catholic Family History Society and the National Catholic Directory. Hopefully I would get a double check on my facts.

Then I took a deep breath, poured a cup of coffee, and turned to the difficult problem of me. I had my birth certificate and a birth year. Was it real? The hospital was real, but most of the folks in the records department had gone home for the day. "Try again tomorrow during business hours," they said. I'd call again, but the chances were probably slim. If I was the child my mother had used in her jewelry store heists, I would have been anywhere from two to five years old. That had me narrowing down the years. I still felt there was a link from my mother to the murdered man, Uncle Mickey. I just had to find it. Somewhere in the depths of the internet were the awaited answers.

I checked the missing children web pages and searched through the state entries for several years. I started with California, the state listed on my birth certificate. I could have been any number of faces; many were blurry. What had I looked like as a child? Had I been blonde? Short? Chubby? My mother had kept no pictures, so I had no sense of reference. What family did not keep pictures of itself? No birthday snaps. No summers at the beach. No proms. I tried to remember if I had ever seen any photo albums lying around the house. Maybe my mother had thrown them all away. Had she even owned a camera? I gave up on speculations and non-memories and tried the missing children pages for several surrounding states over a course of years with no more luck. Some had no photos, just a name and vague description. I could have fit several dozen of the lost faces.

I needed a better strategy. I made a grid list of states and years and started again, marking boxes that seemed possible. I only made it through a few states before darkness had Albie cooing for food and the exhausting day took its toll on my brain.

When I checked my email, I saw that one of the sources for Mary Catherine or Wilma Stone had come through as positive. That cheered me up, but not enough to tackle anything else on the computer.

I knew a car was outside, and the night concierge had been briefed to be on the lookout, but still I double locked the door and wedged a chair under the knob. Then I eased into a steaming bath and tried to blot out the day, my life. I closed my eyes, scrunched down into the hot water, and imagined fluffy clouds and rainbows. I woke up to teeth-chattering cold. No clouds or rainbows. As quickly as I could, I toweled dry, snuggled into the warmest pajamas I owned, covered Albie, and went to bed. The black enveloped me like a womb.

****

Email to Hannah B.

Dear Hannah—

I think I have found her. Wilma Stone appears to have joined a convent in California and taken the name Sister Mary Catherine. Census records bore out the fact, and I got confirmation from one of the Catholic organizations I emailed. I am enclosing the contact information for you. They can give you dates and a location. I'm sorry to say she died several years ago. Attached is a copy of her death certificate. I hope this helps and will bring you some closure to the matter.

Please let me know if you have questions or concerns. If I get further information from other sources, I will let you know.

Thanks,

El

****

The knocking woke me, and I jumped groggy from bed. Peered through the keyhole. It was Poe. I tried to finger brush my hair into shape, but he had seen me in worse shape.

"El, how are you doing? Any contact? Phone calls?"

"No. Do you want coffee?"

"A quick cup."

When I got the coffee pot going, I remembered my discovery. I told him about it as I uncovered and fed Albie. "I found out what the receipt was for—a storage locker. Now I just have to find out which one." I told him the whole story of my journey through the banks.

"Not on your own, you don't. Give me a day to get some things under control, and we can drive around. I need to check on some things anyway. There seems to be a rash of petty theft going on. At first, I thought it was just random, but this might be the work of kids, maybe a gang. Items left outside on porches disappearing, small things lifted from restaurants and offices; I think they might be connected."

"That's annoying. Shouldn't kids be in school this time of year? Maybe it's an older gang?"

"It's kid stuff though: a woman called in that several pots of flowers were taken from her porch, a mother said two of her kids' beach towels were grabbed off the front railing where they were drying, bunches of magazines from waiting rooms, bags of condiments from restaurants, a lawn chair, local stores and pharmacies have reported missing socks and underwear, baby formula, toothbrushes, the list goes on. Each one is not enough to investigate, but together there seems to be a pattern. A pattern of what, I'm not sure. One person complained, and it set off a flurry of reports. Neighbors have been talking. People have begun to call in over any item gone missing. One woman declared her glasses had been stolen only to call ten minutes later to say she had found them. It appears to be concentrated in a good-sized area. I've sent a squad car to do a slow roam of the streets and dispatched a few officers on foot. That's about all I can spare. I do want to check on a few people though."

With a weary sigh, he continued, "The old Chief who retired had planned on establishing precincts in some of the neighborhoods. If we get ahead on the budget, I'd love to be able to do that. Having more localized stations could help deal with issues like this. I always felt having a police presence in neighborhoods was a good thing. People could get to know officers, and police could get to know the people in that area. Anyway, for now, the thefts are one of the problems I must solve. As I said, word has gotten around, and every person who has misplaced even a sock is calling in to report it."

I didn't envy him the job. "You're right. The thefts do sound like kid stuff."

"Listen, let's go talk to Josh at the pet store first and check out storage lockers another day. Did you make a list with addresses?"

"Not yet, and I don't want to burden you with this, but I think that woman that ran into me at the Grady was following me around to each bank. I waited then doubled back and went into each with the story of renting a safety deposit box. That's when one of the tellers recognized the receipt. If you go with me to the storage sites, that mystery woman is sure to see us." I didn't tell him about the picture I had tried to take of her that ended up being a beauty shot of the parking lot asphalt.

"Still, it's the only safe way. Wait for me." He put down his cup and walked to the door. Pointed to all the papers beside my computer. "What have you been doing?"

"On the premise that I might have been the child used in the robberies, I have been trying to find myself. I'm looking through all the missing children state by state for several years. Then I'm going to search the adoption sites."

He cocked his head to one side. "Have you thought of doing a DNA test?"

"Now why didn't I think of that?" I slapped my palm to my forehead. "It's one of the first things I recommend to people. What is wrong with me?"

"Any other memories come popping up?" He put on his hat and paused.

"Yes. While I was in the library, I remembered the carrot scene."

"The carrot scene?"

"Again, it was late at night. I could hear talking. Even though my mother told me not to come into the kitchen, for some reason I snuck close enough to hear. They were talking about carrots. I started to get hungry, so I broke cover and said, 'I want a carrot too.' My mother got angry and hustled me off to bed and shut the door. I couldn't understand why she got so upset about the vegetable. I think now they were discussing carats as in jewels." I told Poe about the notebooks.

"And you never saw any notebooks, and none were in the boxes?"

"No. The woman knew how to be careful."

He rubbed my arm in way of comfort, but I could see his mind was elsewhere. "I'll call later."

I poured myself some coffee, dressed for the day, and went back to the computer. I moved Albie's cage where he could see me. Put on some soothing music to keep him happy. Made a note to send away for a DNA kit. Then got back to searching sites for missing and adopted children. I continued making extensive notes on page, date, picture. One picture I was certain was me turned out to be a boy. With shaggy hair and old cloudy pictures, it was hard to tell.

After a time, I stopped for self-reflection. What would it be like to gain another family? To suddenly have relatives who remembered me? Who were around when I was born? Did I have sisters or brothers? Maybe a mother had been crying herself to sleep for twenty years. Maybe they kept a picture of me on the mantel or wall. Maybe they had my room left as it was when I went missing. What if I had parents and they didn't report me missing? Maybe they didn't care. Maybe they had sold me to my fake mother. Maybe I wasn't really this age. I kept having the same thoughts repeatedly until they clung to me like a suffocating blanket. I had been El Turner for so long, I didn't know if I wanted to be someone else. I had gotten used to being by myself, being independent, relying on my own sense of wellbeing. What if my parents were nutritionists and hated my canned soup and coffee? At least the pumpkin seeds were healthy. Or what if they were gym coaches and found out how unathletic I was? Or singers and found out how scratchy my voice was? The maybes were piling up like fall leaves, and I didn't own a rake. I could drive myself crazy with those heaps of thought.

In the end I was stunned by how many missing children there were. I tried to dismiss the enormity of my situation, but the maybes kept coming, but in the opposite direction, hail stones plinking against the window. Maybe it was a rabbit hole I didn't need to go down. Maybe my mother was really my mother and was playing a trick on me from the grave Maybe she wasn't a thief, but just a saleswoman in a jewelry store. Maybe carrots were just carrots. For anyone else, I would put my head down and do the research, not give way to all this randomness. But I was not anyone else. This might be the most important research of my life. I poured more coffee and wondered if meditation would be a safer choice.

The site for the records building in the state listed on the birth certificate provided contact forms, so I filled them out and sent them off. I also checked every adoption records agency that seemed a possible source. Not sure what could come of it, I printed copies of my birth certificate and sent them off to the most likely as well. It was like rolling the dice of fate. Should I hope for odds or evens?

Poe called before bed, but I had little to report. He sounded tired, so I got off quickly.

I looked out the window and saw the squad car. Still, I put a chair under the doorknob, took a long bath, and went to bed. I dreamt of clowns and woke unrefreshed, the bed sheets a vicious damp tangle about my legs, maniacal laughter echoing in my ears.

****

Email to El Turner
Dear El Turner—
Hello. Your name was given to me by someone who used your services several years ago. She was very happy with the results. I'm afraid my results may not be

to my liking, but I must know the truth. I think I may have been switched at birth. I look nothing like anyone in my extended family in real life or in any pictures. I'm blonde with blue eyes, and they are all dark haired with brown eyes. I am an only child, but I have a ton of cousins. Being blonde, I stand out like a banana in a fruit bowl of blackberries. My parents always assured me there was nothing to my fears, but I'm not convinced. They won't tell me why, just saying a DNA test is a waste of money and I'm being silly. I know they love me and do not want me to get hurt.

Is it possible to get a list of babies born at the hospital on the day I was? That way I can possibly find photos or see if there is something to it.

Sincerely,
Kim Hardee

****

Email to Kim Hardee
Dear Kim:

Thank you for your email. I can certainly understand your concerns and questions. Your email does not state your age, but you sound old enough to be able to handle whatever the truth may be. Before you pay for a thorough search into the matter, I would suggest you have a hard conversation with your parents about this. They may not know how important this is to you. You could also let them know how serious you are about taking a DNA test. It is so easy and inexpensive to do these days. It may be the quickest way to solve the problem.

I hope this will help. If not, please let me know if I can be of further assistance.

Good luck in your search,
El Turner

Chapter 8

The recent email request reminded me I needed to send off for a DNA test for myself. I added it to my current list of things to do. For today, I was ready to go over the adoption sites again in another futile attempt to uncover myself among the missing. I had to find some link between my mother and the dead man. I didn't want to be a person of interest in his murder forever. The police seemed to be at a standstill regarding the matter.

I got up, stretched, looked out the window and saw the police car was not there. I searched up and down the street. Nothing. I tried calling Poe but got no answer. My brain leapt at the thought of freedom, then the fear came back like an ice bath gushing down my spine.

When the phone rang, I jumped from my chair, afraid Poe had read my thoughts of venturing out into the world of sure-to-be trouble.

"Hello. You don't remember, but I called about a week ago. I was a friend of your mother's, and I am very interested in getting my bird back. That bird really does belong to me." It was the poet, Mr. Taylor.

"My mother was listed as the owner, Mr. Taylor. Since she died, the bird belongs to me. Besides, didn't you abandon him at the pet store when you left town?"

"I was just going to be gone temporarily. The man at the pet store misunderstood."

"I'm not sure if I would call being absent all this

time as temporary."

"I hope this doesn't mean I will have to go to court to get the bird back. After all, it was my money that paid for everything like your mother's rent and all the necessities. She really owed me, and the bird would settle that debt."

"Look, Mr. Taylor, I'm very busy at present. Can I have your number? I'll call you back as soon as I can."

"Well, I'm in and out. It's hard to reach me. Why don't I call you back tomorrow? What's a good time?"

I could play vague as well. "I will be in and out as well. Just leave a message on the machine, along with your number, and I'll call back."

"Fine. Good day."

I tried the recall button, but a strange woman answered.

"Hi. I'm looking for Mr. Taylor. I was just talking to him."

"Honey, some man just laid this phone down on the desk here and walked out. Probably a burn phone. Guess it's mine now."

Just as I hung up, I heard a knock at the door. I edged toward it warily, unsure what I might find. Could Taylor have gotten here that quickly? I had my new lock in place, and I didn't want to have to call the locksmith again. I might have to buy stock in the lock company. But when I looked through the peephole, I saw the familiar hat.

"The poet just called," I yelled with relief and excitement the minute Poe walked in. "I checked redial and a woman answered and said he left the phone behind and walked out of the building. What do you think he's up to?"

"Hard to say. Was it about Albie again?"

"Yes. And he said something about taking me to court to gain rights to the bird. He said it should be his since he paid for everything while he was with my mother, but I have the bank account record and it shows she covered the bills."

"I don't think you have to worry much."

"What's up? Visiting me in the middle of the morning. Day off?"

"I had to check out something and thought we could do a quick question session with Josh."

"Great. What happened to the police car?"

"Nothing. We are a bit shorthanded, so I am here to protect you."

"Let me get out of my pajamas, and I will be with you shortly." I tried to make myself presentable, and then finally gave up. I got my coat on before Albie, sensing I was leaving, started in on his *Murder! Murder!* serenade. "Oops. I forgot. We need to drop Albie off at Jenny's."

"Do you realize how many activities Jenny has given up being here for you? She has certainly been quite a friend."

"Yes, I do, and I appreciate it very much. Plus, I think deep down she really likes this cloak and dagger stuff. She thinks you're handsome, and it's a bit more exciting than canasta."

"Now there's a woman with good taste." Poe laughed, seeming more at ease today than he had been.

After dropping Albie off, we drove to the pet store.

"I checked. Both Josh and the manager were out sick or on business the day Albie was taken."

Josh happened to be in. His face broke into a wide relieved smile when he saw me.

"I hope this means you've changed your mind," he said. Then he saw Poe behind me.

"You remember Chief of Police Poe, don't you?"

His shoulders drooped along with his smile.

"Have you come to arrest me?" Josh asked. He sank down into a chair behind the counter and put his head in his hands.

"Now, why would we…" I started to ask, but Poe stopped me with a touch to my arm.

"No arrest for now, Josh. Just a talk. Let's start with what you know."

"I'm so sorry. I don't know what came over me. This is so unlike anything I've ever done." He groaned. "I've never been in any kind of trouble. Never!"

"Just start at the beginning," Poe coached.

"Well, first off, Mr. Taylor kept calling me. He contacted me again a few weeks ago and came by the store. He started to ask a lot of questions about when Albie was here. Wanted to know who had him. Wanted to know if I thought you would sell. Then he got specific but like pretending it was just casual chatter. I said Albie was quite the talker and said the strangest things. He wanted to know what the parrot had said when he was here and if he had said anything odd. It didn't seem suspicious at the time, but the more I thought about it, the weirder it became."

"What did you tell him?"

"I mentioned a few things as well as some numbers he said once. I never could get the bird to repeat them. He got very excited over that and wanted to know if I remembered what they were or what had triggered him saying that. Well, that definitely made me suspicious. It seemed like the numbers were important. I shut up then, told him I couldn't remember any more, and he went away."

"What did you think the numbers were?"

"I didn't know. A lottery number? A Swiss bank account? I thought it might be worth my while to see if I could get the bird back. If not for the numbers, to sell it to Mr. Taylor who seemed like he would pay anything."

When Poe didn't respond, Josh looked up at us. "How did you know it was me?"

"Just a hunch. Why did you do it?" Poe stepped closer to Josh. He shrugged his shoulders and raised his eyebrows to show he knew as little as we did.

"After Mr. Taylor, a man I never saw before came into the shop and asked me to break into El's apartment and steal Albie. He offered me a lot of money. A lot. I was shocked. I told him there was no way, but he became very insistent." He waved his hand around. "As you can see, the business is not exactly booming. That new pet store on the other side of town by the highway is a chain business and has taken a good chunk out of my sales. The man said he would give me half to get the bird, and the other half when I handed the bird to him. He even spread a large bunch of hundred-dollar bills on the counter. I have a pile of unpaid bills. I was desperate."

I looked at Poe, light bulbs going off in our brains.

"Let's start with who the man was," Poe began.

"He never said. He was big, dark hair, meaty face, sharp suit, big gold ring on his finger, reeked of cologne."

"And he told you to steal the bird. Why did he want the bird?"

"He wouldn't tell me. He handed me a map of the apartment building, said he would call the concert man to distract him from the front desk, and allow me to slip into the building and take the stairs. He said to wear a dark sweatshirt with the hood up and dark sunglasses. He pointed out where the cameras would be, so I was to look down."

"Are you talking about Albert, the concierge?" Poe asked.

"Yeah. That's the one. The big man gave me a crowbar and showed me how to pry the door open. I was to wear strong work boots in case I had to kick the door in. He said he would wait in a car a block away in an alley, and I was to bring the bird to him, then he would give me the rest of the money and I could slip away. Easy as pie. No one would know it was me, and I'd have money in hand to catch up. Who would pay that much money for a bird? I knew those numbers had to lead to something important."

"So, you snuck past Albert, broke in the door, and snatched the bird."

"I wore gloves, and it was a good thing I did since I left the crowbar in the hall. I even covered Albie's cage, but he kept yelling, 'Murder!' It attracted so much attention as I was running down the street. One man even reached out to grab my sleeve to stop me, and that concierge man was chasing me, so I put Albie down in the grass and just high-tailed it. I hope I didn't hurt him. I thought I could slip in and out. I forgot how loud Albie can get."

Poe and I looked at each other in silence.

"Am I going to jail?" Josh asked, his head still in his hands. His shoulders shook like he was crying.

"I think what I'd like to do, Josh, is take you to the station so you can write out your statement. Then I'd like you to give some details to our sketch artist, and we'll see if you can't get a good likeness of this guy. Do you want to lock up?"

"You're sending me to lock up? You mean prison? Don't I even get a trial?" He jumped out of the chair, his face white and terrified.

"Easy, Josh. I was just asking you if you wanted to lock up the store before you leave."

"Oh." He gave a half-hearted nervous laugh. "My truck is around back. Can I drive it there or do I have to ride in the squad car?"

"I'll drop Ms. Turner off and then meet you at the station. I think we can trust you won't run off again."

"Yes, sir. I will be there." He seemed to take a shaky breath before continuing, "I live upstairs. The old truck out back is mine. I won't run. I have nowhere to go. Everything I have is tied up in this business."

"That's fine," Poe said. "Do you need to call someone? An assistant?"

Josh shook his head no, then finally looked at me. "I'm so sorry, El. Sorry for all the calls. I figured if that many people were anxious to get the bird, there must be something of value attached. What are the numbers for and why do so many people want them?"

"I guess we would all like to know that," I said. I had been so wrapped in my own life, I hadn't realized how the numbers might affect others.

"It just seemed a quick and easy way to make a few bucks. I must have been out of my mind. El, I will pay for the door and lock. I still have the money that man gave me."

"That might help, Josh." Poe nodded. "If you bring it along, we'll give you a receipt and check it for prints.

If you pay, I don't think Ms. Turner will file a complaint."

I shook my head. "I actually need some more food for Albie." I looked at Poe. "Can I buy some before Josh locks up and leaves?"

"Take what you want. It's on the house," Josh said, gathering his things.

Feeling guilty, I grabbed a bag of bird feed and left my money on the counter next to the cash register.

"That clears up a few things," I declared as Poe drove me home. "It's amazing how things turn out. I had Josh down as a suspect, but I never imagined the story behind his reasoning."

"This case has its fingers in a lot of directions. Who knows where it will lead. I think Josh is a nice guy who got caught up in someone's wickedness."

"I agree." I looked out the window as we drove. "I'm almost afraid to go forward and check out the storage lockers."

"Have you gotten the list made?"

"No."

"Do that and I'll get back to you. I think this is enough for today. I'll take care of Josh and call you later if we need you."

I suddenly thought of something. "Who do you think the mystery man is who hired Josh? And why did he want Albie? And what does he have to do with all this? Do you think he might be the Mister X I threw into the pot of suspects? Maybe he's the one who killed Uncle Mickey."

"You are a questioning sort, aren't you?" Poe laughed.

"Well, I am—"

"A researcher. Yes, I know," Poe interrupted. "But the man is still out there. We don't know his next move, so stay inside! Don't go out to any storage locker without me. Promise, El?"

I held up my hand. "Promise." I sighed. Another day stuck inside. And to think I used to love staying in and communing with my computer. This was a new puzzle I wanted to solve. Wherever it was leading, I knew it might solve a piece of me. Or who the real me was. The journey, however, was scaring the wits out of me.

"I'll talk to you later."

He drove off before I remembered that man sounded like the one I had seen in the window reflection at the Grady Hotel while I was waiting to be arrested. I greeted Albert, used my new lock and key, and retrieved Albie from Jenny. For the first time, I really wished I had a television to watch so I could lie on my couch and forget the outside world existed. It was a first, but I was tired of thinking.

****

I spent the next morning getting the list of storage buildings. How could such a small city have so many? I wrote down the addresses and made a map in order of travel so that we wouldn't be driving back and forth. I was excited to see what would come of it. We could take along some of the blacked-out receipts to see if they matched. For the thousandth time, I wondered what the magic numbers Albie had repeated would open. And what in the world had my mother hidden in a storage unit? The tension was too much; I wanted to go right this minute! One would think after the childhood I had, patience would be at my ready fingertips, but the end was possibly in sight, and I wanted to get on with my life, whatever it turned out to be.

Instead, I stretched, jabbered to Albie, and went through the adoption sites again. I created a page with twelve of the top promising missing children who looked the most like me. I even picked out one that I thought resembled a young me. Jennifer Lind from Wisconsin. I could live with that name, maybe even twin with my neighbor and friend Jenny Lane. This Jennifer had been reported missing in Arizona. The family had been on vacation when she disappeared. When I delved into her case further, however, I saw that she had been found two years after being reported missing. Taken by a relative. Happy to be back with her family.

Crossing her off the list, I made up my own lineup of printouts for Poe to see if he had any ideas. In reality, there were so many children that could be me, I was overwhelmed. If the poet called back, I would ask him if my mother had ever said where she was from. She might have let something slip. At least that would be a start.

The California clerk I spoke with said they had no record of my birth on file. As I had thought, my birth certificate was fake. Maybe I should frame it as a reminder that people lied. Or that nothing was as it seemed.

In the end, I went online and ordered my neighbor Jenny a new teapot set—bright ceramic red with hand painted flowers and matching cups— as a thank you for keeping Albie and watching over me.

It was an edgy day with not much relief, so, of course, it rained. The sky hovered overhead like some dark warlord thundering its rage.

****

Email from Tanya Hearst

Dear Ms. Turner—

You might think this is an odd request, but I think I may have a brother.

To start at the beginning, I am an only child. I grew up in a poor household. My father gambled and drank, so we had no money. We moved around a lot. (At times I thought they might be fugitives from the law.) We stayed in a commune in West Virginia for a while. I am attaching a list of places we lived and approximate dates.

You see, I don't know how old I am. My mother only told me I was born when it was hot. I was born at home and home schooled and didn't have friends. But I always dreamed I had a brother named Nathan. I don't know why I thought that or where I got the name from. Maybe I wanted an imaginary friend.

I know that sounds otherworldly, but I wonder if it is possible to find any information on if I did have a brother or not. Maybe he died as a baby? Maybe my mother had a miscarriage? I know this is not much to work with, but I am sending money to your account. Can you investigate as far as the money goes, and we can discuss if we can go further or if it's a dead end?

Thank you for listening.
Tanya Hearst

****

Email to Tanya Hearst
Dear Ms. Hearst—

Thank you for your email. I do not think those feelings are otherworldly; to you they are real and important. I'll do what I can. Can you tell me which of the places you lived in might be where you were born? That would narrow things down. If you have specific addresses, that might help. Do you have any indication if Nathan was older or younger than you? Do you remember your parents ever changing their (or your) names when moving? Can you also supply me with their first names and middle names or initials if you know them? Last, what was the name of the commune, and where exactly was it located?

I will wait to hear from you.
Best,
El Turner

****

The patrol car was back in front of my building the next day, so I was again a shut in. Even though I had originally wanted to concentrate on my own family tree, I was glad to have outside work to take my mind off my problems. I reread Tanya Hearst's email. How many people were searching for something: a name, a family member, a dream? How many seekers had I helped over the years without giving their pain and anguish much thought? I had built a business on the joy of the hunt and the joy I tried to give them by finding answers. I realized I had always been the solver, not the seeker. Now, as they say, the shoe was on the other foot. I had become both, and the stories had begun to take on a personal tenderness. Tears formed and raced down my face like a burst dam. What was wrong with me?

Suddenly, the computer held no fascination. I didn't even want to sit down in front of it. What changed my love of research was one more question I wasn't sure I wanted to answer. Had empathy pushed its way into my stoic researcher façade?

Wiping away the sentiments from my face, I tried Poe, but he said he would be tied up all day. I put on happy music and tried singing out loud and dancing, scaring Albie into a corner. I wanted to get out and move the case along. I wanted to do something, anything. I wanted to go back to being the me I had always known. How annoying to be so powerless. I felt like a child sent to her room because of bad behavior. Maybe Jenny would like a talk, but she did not answer her door. I guess she figured since the patrol car was in charge, she was free to dally in one of her extracurricular activities. I envied her the freedom.

I stared down the computer, took a deep breath, then finally got back online. With nothing else to do, I kept checking my email, hoping that Tanya Hearst would send me more information. When I searched communes where she might have lived, it was more than I could bear. Too much love and idealism not fit for the real world. My real world anyway.

Rita didn't answer her phone. Probably after a hot story, slinking down NY streets, following enticing leads, free to go where she chose. I left a blathering message.

I did a half-hearted rifle through my mother's boxes again, but nothing new jumped up and waved its arms at me. The papers led nowhere, and the random hodgepodge left behind was worthless. I even checked every pocket, but all I got was lint. In almost all mystery stories I ever read, there was at least a smidgen of a clue to follow. Why could I solve other people's problems but not my own?

When I grew weary of missing children's sites, quixotic communes, and aimless rambling, I checked the games on my computer. Canasta seemed the most enticing. I played for what seemed like hours, but the clock said more like twenty minutes.

While cleaning the kitchen for the third time, I came across the key Dolly had given me. At least if I walked down the hallway I would be out of the apartment. It felt like I was going somewhere, if only just a few yards. I loaded Albie's cage with treats and tiptoed to the door and down the hall to Rita's old apartment.

With my hand on the doorknob, I had second thoughts. I paused before opening the door, convincing myself I was not breaking into someone's home because that was what it felt like, even momentarily. She had given me the key; she wanted me to check on her plants. As much as Rita had spent time in my apartment, I realized I had never once entered hers. I pushed the door open.

All the blinds were closed except for one window, casting the room in dust and shadow. A few boxes lined one wall. I walked gingerly around the sparse furniture the management put in most of the apartments, the same furniture I had lived with and not cared about. Most of the people in the building took unfurnished places and brought their own décor with them.

I walked over toward the light. Two white hairy cacti were sunbathing. Both looked like they were having a bad hair day. Thin wispy filaments shot out at all angles or coiled around the green bodies. One was taller and thinner, probably the old man. I'd have to ask Dolly when she got home. Now that I was here, I didn't know what to say, but talking to Albie had made me comfortable talking out loud.

"I know we haven't been properly introduced, but I'm El. I live just down the hall. Dolly is away now, but she asked me to look in on you. I'd try to pet you or touch you in some way, but I'm afraid of those thorns I think might be under all that hair." I pulled over a chair from the kitchen table that looked a lot like mine.

"You don't know it, but my good friend Rita used to live here. She was a journalist for the local paper. Then she became a person of interest when one of her sources got killed. She got me involved, then I met Poe, and we ended up solving the case. Along the way I got locked in a labyrinth of a basement, found an old journal written by the founder of Parkville, and discovered a bunch of stolen money." I looked around me just to make sure no one was really there and continued. "Well, that was the event in a nutshell. Anyway, I think I can still feel Rita's vibe in this apartment. She was a constant talker, so if you get lonely, listen hard and you will hear echoes of one of her rants." I laughed out loud. Since they were in a listening mood, I told them all about my past job doing research for a television show, how my mother wasn't my real mother, and how I had come across a dead man who said he was my uncle. It felt therapeutic to talk about it. Nothing was any clearer, but I felt lighter somehow.

"Okay. It's time to go. I know my bird is probably freaking out. Nice to meet you. Same time next week?" I asked, laughing at the joke.

I walked back down the hallway, unlocked my door, and stepped inside. Just that little reprieve had alleviated my boredom and confinement. Albie looked startled when I walked in. He was still busy with the treats. Now that I was wound up talking to things that could not talk back, I had a long one-sided conversation with Albie while he ate, apologizing for the music, the singing, and the dancing. I then ran through all my theories of who I might be until he burrowed his head in his feathers and pretended to be asleep.

I covered his cage and went to bed. Even a soothing hot bath did not appeal. Poe didn't call. I didn't have any dreams. The world hung still as a star.

****

Email to El Turner

Dear El—

Thank you so much for your advice! I sat down with my parents and told them my reasons for wanting to do a DNA test. Well, long story short, they finally told me the truth. I was not switched at birth as I had feared. It turns out my mother used a sperm donor, and they were afraid to tell me. I had the feeling they didn't want to have to talk about sex to me and explain why they had to use the donor process, but they told me everything. I'm happy to have an answer and feel more at ease with my family now. My father (he will always be my father!) even asked me if he should dye his hair blonde to make me happier.

Thank you!
Kim Hardee (age 16)

****

Email to Kim Hardee

Hi Kim:

I am so happy you got an explanation that eases your fears! Sometimes we let worry and confusion take over our lives when a simple answer is within reach. It sounds like you have a loving family.

Enjoy them!
El Turner

Chapter 9

I stayed in bed long past my usual waking. I could hear Albie chittering away for his breakfast, despite all the goodies I had piled in his cage last night. The day stretched before me as exhausting as a line for a favorite ride at an amusement park. When even the bed seemed to be sick of me, I rose and uncovered Albie. He acted like he was starving although a few stale treats still littered the bottom of his cage. Feeling guilty, I changed the paper, refilled his regular food, and freshened the water.

Pulling the curtains aside, I sighed and looked out to see what kind of day it was. Dim and cloudy as my mood. I glanced down at the street: the police car was gone. I rubbed my eyes. Could it be?

Excitement bubbled up in me like Christmas morning. I couldn't wait any longer to check the storage sites. I was as antsy as a bear waking from hibernation and hungering for his first meal. All my life I had been a quiet, controlled person. My days doled out in measured activity, I had been content with who I was and how I lived. When I had found out my mother wasn't my real mother, I held a long debate with myself about researching my own family tree. It had proved harder than I thought. Now that I was close to finding out answers, I felt like I was riding an unshackled freight train, holding on for dear life. I'm sure neither Poe nor

Jenny could understand the urgency in me, and I'm not sure I understood it myself, but tossing safety and common sense aside, I had to do something. I knew I was going out on a limb. When Poe didn't call by noon, I gathered the pepper spray, a knife, the Albie numbers, and a large sack, for what I didn't know, but it seemed like a good idea.

With his sixth sense, Albie figured out my plans and began to squawk. Treat bribes did not work; he had grown sick of them. I knocked on Jenny's door and was delighted to find her at home.

"Can you watch Albie for a short while?"

"El, where are you off to today? Inspector Poe said to order you to stay home."

"It's just a quick trip for research, Jenny." I was hoping she would assume I was going to the library. "My job does call for research beyond my computer, you know."

"Well, I guess it's okay. Maybe I should check with Inspector Poe." It seemed like she had specific orders. I wondered if she had him on speed dial. "Maybe I should go along," she worried.

"It won't be long. I promise." I tried my puppy dog eyes and a convincing tone. "And if you talk to Chief of Police Poe, tell him I'm fine."

"Just keep your phone on."

"I will." I was about to promise again but didn't want to overplay my hand. I gathered Albie's cage, treats, and food, and went back down the hall. "Here he is!"

"Oh, look at that handsome boy," Jenny cooed. If a parrot could simper, Albie would have done it.

I said my farewell and turned back to the apartment.

I had another idea. "Jenny," I called before she had fully closed her door. "Would you mind if I borrowed your car? I hate to ask it, but my tires seem a bit low, and I don't want to get a flat. I was going to see about getting an appointment, but with all that's been going on…" I left the sentence hanging.

"No problem at all," Jenny said, handing me the keys.

If someone was following me, they wouldn't recognize her car. I put on a hooded sweatshirt, which seemed to work for other people avoiding detection, deciding at the last minute to take down the horrible painting Rita had left me and put it in the sack. If one of the storage facilities seemed right, I could pretend to put the painting in storage. I also rummaged through my junk drawer and found an old lock. At the last minute, I remembered the receipts. I put a few in the bag. Halfway down the stairs, I checked my pockets and realized I had forgotten the list of facilities.

"Get it together!" I whispered to myself. I crept back past Jenny's door and silently retrieved the list. When I was convinced I had everything I needed, I hid behind a column in the garage and checked out the surroundings. No one seemed to be stalking the shadows or waiting in a car. Nevertheless, I put up my hood, lowered my head, and changed my walk to a sort of loping limp I hoped would fool anyone watching for me.

Jenny's neon green compact stood out like a clown at a church service, but I knew no one would connect it to me. Still, I checked my mirrors to make sure. I sped up at times or slowed down, weaving in and out of traffic. Then I pulled over at a gas station and concentrated on the passing cars. When I felt safe, I proceeded to the first storage lot on my list.

****

The place was smaller than I expected, but I was glad to see surveillance cameras when I drove in. I put up my hood, went into the office, and asked the woman behind the desk if I could see a sample unit. She locked the door of the office and walked to a nearby shed. As she opened the door, I asked about security.

"We have the usual cameras, a high fence, and gate that closes at ten each night."

"Is someone in the office all the time?" I asked while peeking around the bare walls metal unit.

"I'm afraid not. We've got the cameras and have never had a problem."

"What sorts of locks do most people use?" I was stalling for time as I attempted to glance at the road to see if anyone had followed me.

She gestured for me to walk back to the office with her. There she showed me various locking devices. "We sell some of these, but most people bring in their own."

I thanked her, showed her the blacked-out receipt, but she shook her head. I looked around at the street then got back on the road. By the fourth storage site, I was thoroughly tired of viewing plain metal buildings with concrete floors. Tired of having managers dismissing the old receipt.

By the time I got to the next one, I was ready to call it a day. I had been longer than I told Jenny I would be gone. I checked my phone, but no one had called. *Just one more,* I said to myself. I checked off the address on the list and prepared to get out. A jolt went through me as if I stuck my finger in a light socket.

I took out the paper that held Albie's numbers. Sure

enough! The three numbers in the storage address matched the first numbers in Albie's recitation. My hand was shaking. Why had I not noticed that when I was compiling the list of sites? Some researcher I was. And an even worse investigator.

I was afraid to get out of the car. Should I call Poe and wait for him to come help? My trembling fingers refused to punch in the right numbers. They slipped off keys and danced away like naughty children. When I finally got through, it was his voicemail that answered. I hung up without a message.

Ever cautious now that I was nearer to the ultimate destination, I put up my hood, donned my sunglasses, and went into the office. The manager was a wiry man with a hyper attitude and disapproving scowl, as if he thought the world was out to cheat him. I showed him the blacked-out receipt.

"Is this one of your receipts?"

"Yeah," he grunted. "Where did you find it? In a gutter?"

I tried the honest approach, trying to look naive. "My mother died last year, and this was in her possession. I'm trying to see if she had rented a storage unit here."

"Name?" He picked up an old record book.

"My name?"

He looked up with pinched exasperated lips and spoke slowly as if to a child. "No, her name."

"Lizzie Turner. It might be Elizabeth."

He took his time. I noticed there were several video cameras on the wall. Not all of them seemed to be working.

"Got nothing under that name."

"Are you sure?"

He put his arms on the counter and leaned my way, heavy tattoos on display. "Are you?"

My mother must have used another name. I had grown weary of her games.

"Well, I would like to rent a storage shed, please."

He looked me over and stared at the green VW outside. "How long?"

"How long is the storage shed?"

He dropped to the child-speaking voice again, drawing out each word. "How long do you want to rent the shed for?"

"Oh, sorry. This is the first time I've rented a storage unit. After my mother died, I have these boxes I want to store until I move. I just don't want things to be broken or to get wet. You know how movers can be." Why in the world was I prattling on to this man? I sounded like a first-class idiot. "One month, please."

"Name and address?"

My mother's daughter at last, I gave him a fake name and address. I could hear Poe having kittens as I spoke.

He quoted a price, took my money, and gave me a receipt, not unlike the one I had from my mother. I saw she had blacked out the name, address, and phone number of the place. Also, the storage unit. He pointed down a row of large metal buildings to one not far from the office.

"Do you have any other units?"

"Only one available. Unit number 12."

"Is it okay to walk around? Get a feel for the place?"

He looked at me as if I had asked for a slice of green cheese. "No skin off my ass."

"I just wanted to let you know in case you see me on the security cameras."

"Most don't work," he said, shrugging and getting back to whatever video game he had been playing on the computer when I came in.

I drove to the unit and unloaded the bag I had packed with Rita's horrid old picture. I was glad to have it out of the apartment. The storage unit had a door that opened upward, like a garage door. I left it open in case someone was watching. Several cars went by, and I waved. I pretended to be looking through the sack.

I checked my notebook with the numbers Albie had spouted: 145 664 823 144. The address of the storage lot was 145 Clark Hill Road. That took care of the first three numbers. My storage unit was number 12, so the chances were good my mother's unit could be 66. The numbering seemed odd. That left several numbers too many for whatever lock she had put on the unit.

I stopped before walking around to test my theory. I called Poe again but got his voicemail. I couldn't even imagine how angry he would be when he found out what I was doing. My hands began to tremble like they were in their own personal earthquake. I was a mix of giddy and hysterical. It was now or never. I put the old lock I had brought onto my unit door and spun the dial. What was the combination? Damn. Too late now. I hoped I had the number in the same drawer where I found the lock. If not, Rita's painting was prisoner in unit number 12. I just hoped Rita wouldn't visit any time soon and ask where it was.

Once more, I was using a painting to divert attraction. I thought about Rita. I wished she were here. My partner in crime. She'd have some crazy idea or two.

When I could wait no longer, I moved away from my unit and began walking around the rows of lockers. I left Jenny's car parked next to number 12. Anyone driving by on the highway could see it. It was a fairly busy place. Several people were loading and unloading things from their lockers, but they did not look suspicious. One family's kids were playing Frisbee and running around with a dog.

I didn't find unit 66. The numbers didn't seem to make sense. Suddenly I came upon a 664, which almost had me yelling in excitement when I noticed the door had an old lock. This must be it!

It took all my frazzled nerves to calm my walk to a stroll back to Jenny's car. The slow walk did provide one revelation. I had been in such a hurry to find my mother's locker, I hadn't noticed that my unit was between 122 and 126. Obviously, the number 4 had fallen off my unit and not been replaced. When the man in the office had said unit 12, I had just assumed the fact. The researcher in me shook her head in disgust. Don't assume facts. Double check.

When I was sure it was safe, I walked back toward the 664 unit. The padlock looked to be hardened steel with a possible three-or four-digit combination. I had 823 144 to work with, never imagining there would be so many choices. Eight seemed like the first number since the dial didn't go up to eighty-two, but was the next one a two or a three or a twenty-three? It didn't help that my hands couldn't sit still. I lost track of which combinations I had used. I should have written my attempts down. Nothing seemed to work. Who knew what traps my mother had set?

No one seemed to be around, so I sauntered back

down my row to Jenny's car just where I had left it. I opened the door and sat inside, frazzled to the bone. I looked again at the numbers. Where did I go wrong? I tried to think like my mother, but through fear and nerves, I was no match. Perhaps the best solution was to go home, tell Poe about it, and wait until he could come back.

Once I made the plan, I started the car. When the ignition sparked, so did I. What if the first number was right, but the others needed to be added together in some fashion. I took out my pen and paper and wrote down eight. Then I added two and three to get five. As I wrote down eight-five, my heart suddenly felt like it had a defibrillator attached. I realized that was the start of my birthday: August fifth. My birth certificate listed August fifth, 1989. With shaking hands, I added the last three numbers. They added up to nine.

The past came rushing back clear as a river. I saw the piece of paper—an application to a boarding school or camp or some sort—with my name written last name first: Turner, Lana. In the space for middle name, she had put an X.

"Is my middle name X?" I had asked. A middle name was not something I had ever considered.

She laughed. "No, X is not your middle name. When you have a blank space, you can put an X. Besides, your name is special enough. You don't need anything more."

"But I want X as my middle name," I had pouted. It suddenly sounded thoroughly intriguing.

"Okay," she had conceded. "You can have X as your secret identity middle name."

I loved the idea.

"But remember that secret identities are just that,

secret."

"Why is my name Turner, Lana?" I was full of questions, even back then.

"Sometimes forms ask for the last name first."

"So, I am Turner, Lana?"

"On here you are."

It didn't make sense, but I accepted it as one more unknown rule of the world.

Several days later, I had headed my homework assignment with my name as Turner, Lana X and the numbers 8-5-9. Even though my mother taught me at home, I still had to put my name on the homework.

"I thought we were keeping that name a secret?" she had asked. "And if these numbers are for your birth date, they should be written 8-5-89. The year usually has two numbers."

I had taken her hand and led her to our telephone, an old landline we rarely used. I pointed to the numbers. "The number 8 has a T under it for Turner, the number 5 has an L under it for Lana, and the number 9 has an X under it for my secret middle name. So, 8-5-9 is both my birthday and my secret identity," I said proudly.

She had looked at me long and hard, and I thought at first she was going to yell or add more pages to my homework, but she suddenly smiled and laughed, clapping her hands. "That's amazing, kid. I see something of me has rubbed off on you." She went to the cupboard and took out two glasses which she filled with grape juice. "Here's to secret identities." She had clinked her glass gently against mine.

Now I felt like I was at a crossroads of the past and the present. Was this bit of trickery meant as a clue for me or a method of distraction for others? Had she adopted my secret code as hers? And why would she be leaving me clues? Mother she might have been, but benefactor she was not. I doubted she would leave anything to me.

Trying to keep my wits about me, I got out of the car, ambled back along the rows, and stopped in front of 664. No one was around. The Frisbee family had gone. I crossed my fingers and gave the lock a whirl.

The click when it came sounded like an explosion. Now that I was here, caution returned like a shrieking alarm clock. I knew there were video cameras around, but which ones worked and how much did the manager watch? My hunch was that he was either sleeping, playing games, or doing things in the back which I didn't want to think about.

My hands decided to stop working altogether, and I dropped the lock when I pulled it away. I thought I heard a scraping, but no one seemed to be about. Who knew what was inside? I hoped it wasn't a bunch of boxes to go through. Maybe the unit was full of priceless artwork. Antiques. Jewels hung from the rafters. The metal door lifted slowly upward. My mind was shooting off fireworks and screaming yippees and yahoos. I had never been this excited before. My feet couldn't feel the ground.

The inside was an utter disappointment, my hopes body slammed to the concrete floor as if by some manic-muscled wrestler. I opened the door halfway, so no one would see inside without bending. In a corner of the building was a single desk. No chair. No papers. No bejeweled rafters. Just a chewed up old-timey office desk. The only light was from outside. I pulled the door back down a bit, just enough so I could see. I wish I had brought a flashlight. Hadn't I learned anything?

I cautiously made my way over to the desk. The top was worn and gouged by pen and pencil marks. Some initials. I tugged on the top drawer. It was locked; all the drawers were locked. Should I pry them open? After all, it was my mother's and I had inherited her things. Would a court agree with me, or would I be arrested again for unlawful entry? It wasn't hard to jimmy the drawer. I used a nail file in my purse. My breath stilled, dumb as dishwater. The drawer was filled with old dusty schoolbooks. I pulled them out and set them on top of the desk. I couldn't wait to see what secrets waited inside. I opened the other drawers the same way. Faded notebooks, chewed up pencils, worn erasers. What was going on? Was this my mother's idea of a joke? One more jab from the grave? If she had still been alive, I might have strangled her. With every tentative step up, there was a crashing down.

Well, I was here now. I thought back to spy shows I had seen. I then took each book, leafed through the pages, and shook them over the desk. Nothing. I remembered one movie where the first letter of certain words was underlined to reveal a name. There were no underlined letters. Maybe it had something to do with the titles. If it did, I couldn't break the code. I searched the notebooks for clues. They weren't even her notebooks. All I found out was that Sheri loved Billy. She had drawn enough hearts and arrows to make that perfectly clear.

I wiped away the dust and sat down on a corner of the desk. I examined the treasures I had amassed. What was my mother's game? I had felt so excited to be able to follow her clues, but now, surrounded by fusty, decaying schoolbooks, I felt like the class dunce. At least there were enough corners in the building to stand in.

I thought I heard a car close, but the busy road was nearby. I feared opening the door more or closing it completely.

I saw the shadow on the concrete floor before I saw the person. I jumped away from the desk like I had been stung by a whirl of hornets.

"What are you doing down here?" the manager yelled, pushing the door open further. "I rented you another unit. Are you stealing stuff? I'm calling the police."

"No, please don't. I showed you the receipt I had from my mother. I do legally own this since my mother left all her possessions to me."

"How'd you know how to open the lock?" He waved his arm at the desk. "And what's all this stuff?"

I jabbered on with the first thing that came to my mind. "This is the desk I had when I was in grade school, and these are all my books and notebooks. My mother was very sentimental and loved to keep things of mine." I almost choked on that last part.

He seemed to be unbending, so I prattled on. "I can show you all the things I had from school. Maybe you want to hear some of the poems I wrote in grade school. You can look at some of the notes I made in my history book."

"Ah, no." He hedged away. "Just wanted to let you know I'm shutting the office for a bit. Gates will still be open to go in and out, but I won't be available for about an hour." He seemed to have forgotten the part about how I opened the lock.

"Okay. Thank you." I waited a minute then peeked out the door and watched him walk back to the office. I sank against the metal wall. Put my forehead against the cool steel ridges. Nothing had changed. I was a total wimp at intrigue. Go home and call Poe, my brain screamed, but my heart nudged me onward. I pulled the door back down so I couldn't be easily seen.

I didn't know where to go from here. I walked around the inside, but nothing else was there. I traced my hand along the ridges. Nothing on the wall or door. No invisible ink or pointing arrows. I walked back to the desk. Once more, I went through the task of delving into each funky book and worn notebook. I shook the pages to make sure no secret code or message was inside. Jiggled the pencils and pens to make sure nothing was hidden. I even tried to take the erasers out to see if jewels were stuffed inside the pencils. If there were diamonds here, I could not guess where they would be. Had someone already found what my mother had hidden? If that had been the case, the lock would not have been so rusty.

As I shook one book, several of the pages tore clear from the spine and spiraled to the floor. Just to be thorough, I got down on my knees on the concrete floor. It looked like someone had kept a car here, and it had leaked oil or other fluids. My hands and knees were filthy. I felt around under the desk for the paper. Scratched my arm. Bumped my head. Something got caught in my hair. Fearing the worst, I jerked my head away, brushing fingers across the top of my hair. Who knew what creatures were crawling around? I hoped no spiders had taken up residence. Cautiously, I felt around underneath the desk.

When I found the package, it was smaller than I imagined. At first, I thought it was some fuzzy mold growing on the underside of the desk. It felt soft and velvety. The parcel was fastened by duct tape. I pried it off. The black velvet bag felt lumpy. I should have known. It was imprinted with her beverage of choice.

I bumped my head once more for good measure and pulled myself up using the desk. My knees were not happy. I took the tape off the bag and unknotted the golden draw cord. My god! What if there were diamonds? I should call Poe immediately. I opened the bag and peeked inside. Things glittered.

I reached into my purse for my phone just as I saw a large figure duck under the door.

"Yes?" I hid the bag behind me. I thought the manager had left. What could he want now? The figure turned to the side and a sliver of light caught his face.

"Uncle Mickey?" My voice echoed in the stunned stillness.

Chapter 10

"Not quite, my dear."

"But I saw you die." I stuttered. "You can't be alive."

"I'm alive, sweetheart. My brother is not."

On inspection, I squinted my eyes and saw that he was taller, a bit more trimmed around the waist, wore a sharp brown suit and crisp white shirt. Nothing like the musty tweed coat. But the features were close.

I took a moment to digest that. Not another brother duo. What was life doing to me? Then it hit me; he was the man I had seen in the window at the crime scene. The one who had disappeared when I turned around.

"You're the man who paid Josh to steal Albie. I saw you at the Grady too. Were you there to see who killed your brother?" I had gained a bit of sense and was moving closer to my purse. Maybe I could get to the phone or pepper spray.

For an answer, he took out a small gun. "Guesses are open."

"You! You killed your brother. You were on the scene." I hoped to stall for time.

"So were a lot of people," he replied, the gun still trained on me. "You, for instance. I saw you with the body. You found him. Very suspicious."

"Why would I kill him?"

"I could ask the same question. I'm interested in one

thing. The item in your hand right now. So why don't you just give me that bag and I might let you live."

"If you killed your brother, what chance do I have?"

"Well, that's a good point." His chuckle was low and dark. "That is *if* I killed my brother. I'm not admitting anything, sweetheart. The last time I confessed, I was ten years old."

"How did you find me? I was so careful."

"Yeah. You're pretty good switching cars, all the dodging in traffic, going to all those places. But I'm good too. Been doing it a lot longer as well. Plus, that bright green car is a dead giveaway." He snickered. "Dead, all right. Seems fitting, don't you think?"

"Since both of us probably will not make it safely out of here, why not tell me the whole story. Your brother was going to. An exchange for what's in this bag."

"You think you have a bargaining chip? I could just as easily shoot you right now and take it."

"Maybe. Someone might hear you. Noise echoes in here. And there's cameras outside." I tried to bluff any way I could.

"Nice try. I caught the guy just as he was leaving. I've been in the office and seen that the cameras don't all work. Who do you think took my money to keep quiet about what number unit you rented? He also sang about this one. He took the money and headed straight for the gates before locking up the office."

"A shot would give you away. People would hear," I repeated, grabbing at straws.

"No one close. I'll take the odds."

He looked around and gauged the situation.

"How did you find it?" he asked.

"Find what?"

"The rocks. And don't get cute with me, honey."

"A little birdie told me."

"Yeah, I tried to pay that pet store guy to get the bird, but he was sloppy. He told me about Lizzie's boyfriend. That jerk was an easy mark. Easy to make talk. He suspected Lizzie had given the locale to the bird. He overheard her a time or two, but he had no idea what the numbers were. She was a real cagey sort though, your mother. I have to hand it to her. She didn't take any chances. Always trying to set traps and false trails."

"I found out about Lizzie, but I never heard about you. Where do you fit? If Uncle Mickey was her brother, then you must be as well." I hoped if I could keep him talking someone might wander by. Why hadn't I told Poe where I would be? Stupid! Stupid!

"I guess you can't smell a crock of lies, can you? He was no blood to your mother. Mick, or Uncle Mickey, or whatever he called himself, let me in on the score. Sure, he was my brother, but we didn't run in the same circles. Hadn't seen him in years. Then he calls me out of the blue. I hardly knew him; he was in such bad shape. He went on and on about being on a treasure hunt and getting what was due him. Let it slip when he had one too many one night. Crying in his beer, as they say, which he seemed to be doing quite often. He told me what a tight group they were until your mother ran off with the diamonds. I couldn't tell if he was more broke up about her or the lost jewels. My sources tell me Finn's in town as well joining the search." He stopped and moved closer to the door, his face more in the shadows. "Since you're a nosy kind, I figured you latched on to the Dixies and their activities. Lizzie kept the last score all to herself. A massive one too. Skipped out on Finn and Mick without giving them their share. Guess it was too tempting after all these years." He lifted the gun and aimed it.

I stood still, afraid of what was to come. Then I saw movement outside. Was the manager back? Could Poe have found out where I was? Another thought surfaced—maybe it was the woman member of my mother's gang here to do us both in. I tried to think of more to say to distract him, but my mind had gone blank as a massive snow drift.

"I heard about the pepper spray you carry, so I don't want to get too close." He looked ready to make a quick exit. "Why don't you ease away from your purse and then just toss that extremely rich goodie bag very gently my way and we'll see what happens."

"But—"

"No buts. Do it now!"

I was going to tell him that the bag was open, and if I threw it, who knew what would happen. An idea was forming. I stretched my fingers to make sure the bag was wide open and then slowly tossed it so it would rotate in the air. It was better than I imagined. Diamonds sprayed out like drops of shiny dew. Even in the dimness, they sparked and glinted and threw fairy lights all over. It was like a world of stars was alive and dancing. He was as stunned as I was.

I heard him swear as he reached out and tried to catch some out of the air. It sounded like rain when the diamonds pelted the concrete.

"Thought you were smart, huh? Why don't you get down on your knees and gather them up for me? Here's the bag back." He picked it up and tossed it to me. "On your knees. Now."

I moved away from the desk and began to pick up the jewels, ignoring the bits of dirt and leaves on the floor. It wasn't easy in the dimness. I kept having to wipe my fingers on my clothes to get rid of the gunk.

"Hurry up. I don't have all day!" He bent down and began to gather them and put them into his suit pocket. He put the gun under his arm. "Don't get any ideas. I'm still one of the best shots around."

I saw the form outside become reality. In a flash, a slim figure ducked down under the door and kicked out at him from behind, catching the back of his knee and sending him sprawling. He tried to rise, but the figure came around and drop kicked him against the wall. His head hit the metal with a thud, the gun clattering to the floor and skidding away.

"Quick, El, grab the gun before he moves."

****

I swallowed my disbelief. "Rita?" I felt like I was in a dream. "Rita? Is that you? What in the world? How did you know? What?"

"Yes, it's me. Grab the gun. It looks like he's out, but we won't know for how long." When she saw I wasn't moving, she poked at his leg with her foot then came over and picked up the gun.

"I guess it's better if I hold it. We don't want you to shoot yourself in the foot on top of everything else."

"Rita!" I kept repeating the questions. "How did you get here? What are you doing here? How did you manage to send him flying into the wall? Am I dreaming this?"

"Well, hello, my friend. Good to see you too." She stood backdropped with light behind her like some sort of superhero then came over, walking gingerly around the gems, and gave me a big hug. "You do remember I live in New York, right? I thought I mentioned that Reb had me take all those self-defense courses. He also taught me how to shoot."

"But how did you know I was here?"

"Jenny told me. She described her car. I just missed you as you left the parking garage. I tried to follow you but lost you somewhere along the line. You were zigzagging all over the place. I turned around and backtracked. I drove up and down the road looking for her car, then I saw it from the highway. It sure is hard to miss."

"I was afraid it was too showy and would attract attention, but now I'm glad it did. It seems everyone was following me, and here I thought I was being clever. I'm a failure at spying."

In the distance we heard sirens. "Oh, and by the way, this time, I *did* call Poe. I learned that lesson the hard way if you remember." She breathed over her fingertips and rubbed them on her leather jacket. "The boys in blue should be here any minute. You can fill me in while we collect these diamonds."

"Oh, Rita!" I plopped down on the oily diamond-littered floor and blubbered like I was drowning.

****

"Well, that was the best home-cooked meal I've ever had!" Rita patted her stomach and leaned back in her chair. "Harry and I usually go out to eat. And I can't believe I see a real table here. It used to be covered in computer and papers and all sorts of scribbling. You even have matching plates. I leave for a little while and you become domesticated." She giggled. "Anyway, I commend the chef and the décor."

It had taken us a few days to recover from the storage building fiasco and oodles of time vacationing in a police interview room. Tonight was a time of laughter and Poe's wagging finger. It had taken that long for me to get used to the new Rita. She was a whole different person—confident, sharp, organized. Her hair shone with a muted redness instead of that brassy color. The layered cut was stylish, and her clothes looked well-tailored.

"I guess I've come a ways from canned soup." I laughed, thoroughly enjoying the sight of my friend in my apartment again.

"Thank goodness," Rita and Poe cried at the same time.

"And who in the world is Harry?" I narrowed my eyes and smiled.

"My editor. Nothing there. Just friends." She winked. "So far."

"Yes, I heard Officer Wilson had moved to New Orleans. That's quite a change for him," Poe said.

"Actually, he wanted to go. We were both always so busy, it seemed like a relationship was not in the cards. When he got the chance to transfer, he did." Rita played with her fork.

"So, what is it like being back in Parkville?" Poe asked. "Do you miss the slower-paced life?"

"No offense to Parkville and all its homey residents, but I love the big city. What energy! I fit right in. I've had some whopper stories I've gotten to cover. I can't tell you how thrilling that is."

"Yes, El keeps a scrapbook with all your bylines in it," Poe said.

"You do? El, you really do?" Rita looked astounded.

"Of course. You know what a junkie I am for newspapers, and you are my favorite journalist."

"I could cry," Rita sniffed, but turned her look into a broad smile.

"Now there's the Rita I used to know."

"I'm horrified to look at those old pictures of mine—the hair, the makeup, the flashy clothes. What was I thinking?"

"Well, you're a sleek city woman now," I said.

"I guess we both have changed a lot." Rita squeezed my hand. "No matter how much either of us changes, you will always be the sister I never had."

Her words surprised me. Other than the surface changes to the furniture and the apartment, I still felt like the same old El Turner.

There was a pause in the conversation. "I'll make coffee," Poe said.

"He seems right at home." Rita winked, cocking her head to the side. "I guess your blush says it all. I mean it. You smile more. You've got a wonderful softness to you now that you never had before. It suits you."

I tried to change the subject. "Did you have flashbacks yesterday when we were asked to make statements?"

"At least this time we didn't have to coordinate our facts," she whispered. "And there will not be a trial, so we won't have to testify. Even with all the publicity, which you know I love, I couldn't handle another one of those. Poe said the statements we signed as well as the jewels in hand should be enough to hold him."

"This is all so unreal what with another set of brothers and a knife. I've had enough of that as well. Someone please tell me this is a dream."

"Do you think he's the killer? Is it Deja vu?"

"He danced around that answer. Said he wasn't admitting to anything. I hope he is, so the heat is off me."

"Amen."

I looked at my friend and smiled. "So how has your time back home been? Did you meet with Bradley Washington, your old editor?"

"It was wonderful. After all the business at the police station, I went back to the hotel, slept for a day, and then he took me to dinner. Today, I went around and visited. Talked to Jenny for a bit. What fun! Now here I am back at my second home." She got up and walked around. "I see you got a new sofa. I like it. And a footstool. I don't see my painting though. Do you still have it?"

I cursed and reprimanded myself for not putting it back on the wall. It was still hanging around storage unit 12. "The hook came loose. I took it in for a new frame. Don't want your art crashing to the floor."

She walked over to the cage. "Albie, my old friend. Do you remember your pal, Rita?"

Albie bobbed his head up and down. "Rita! Rita! Rita!"

"Oh, he remembers me."

"Yes, I'd much rather he yells your name than murder."

"I don't understand." Rita came back and sat at the table just as Poe brought the coffee and cups out.

"El's had a break-in or two since you left. One person tried to run off with Albie. The bird started screeching that word and alerted the whole city.

"Okay, we have a whole pot of coffee. Tell me what's going on." She looked around at us. "Off the record."

"It appears my mother, or so-called mother, was a jewel thief. Diamonds."

Albie spouted the numbers. We had them memorized by now.

"Oh crap. We found out there are certain words we can't say around Albie. D-i-a-m-o-n-d-s is one of them. It seems that the man who was killed originally was the fence she and her partner used. They had all sorts of disguises and traveled the country robbing jewelry stores and museums. At some point my mother felt they needed to change their MO and I came into the act."

"Who was the man killed? Did he have a name?"

"He said his name was Mick Taylor, but I'm finding it hard to believe. Anyway, he dealt in the stolen merchandise and got a percentage. My mother absconded with their last heist, a large load of the white stuff. Uncle Mickey and my mother's partner tried to track her down for years, but she kept on the move. She had learned how to be crafty. When she settled here, they found her. Her death certificate rang some bells. I didn't know that placing a small obit in the paper would set off such a commotion. My 'uncle' cornered me in the park and tried to feel me out about the heist, luring me to the hotel by saying he had info on her. The other woman sniffed around pretending, we think, to be a cleaning woman, following me around town, and keeping tabs on my movements."

"And the man with the gun?"

"The man you so brilliantly kung-fu-ed said he was the dead man's brother."

Rita pretended to take a bow. "I might just have to let Reb know about that. Tell him his prodding was put to good use."

"The woman is still at large," I continued. "Now that the jewels are in police custody, do you suppose she will stop her attacks? Put the whole thing to bed?"

"I doubt it." Poe sat back down and refilled our cups. "I'd say it's not over yet. She might not know the jewels have been found. We're trying to keep it out of the papers. She's still a person of interest in Uncle Mickey's death. She was on the spot and had blood on her. We have not been able to talk with her, mostly because we don't know what she looks like, so she's still at large and presumed dangerous.

"Also, Uncle Mickey's brother is not confessing. He has adamantly denied killing anyone. In fact, El, his story is that your mother stole the jewels from him and now you were trying to hide them."

"But what about holding me at gunpoint?"

"He said you threatened him with pepper spray, and he was just trying to protect himself."

"What?" Rita and I cried at the same time.

"No worries. I got a call from a certain government agency that they are taking over. The stones might be tied to an international robbery."

"They can't find him guilty on that. I doubt he was the one to steal them. Will they just let him go?"

"If they can find no connection or he has an alibi, they will send him back to us. I have a feeling though they might find other reasons to hold him."

"I'm sure he killed his brother. And what about the hotel manager? Isn't he still a person of interest? There must be other suspects. I don't want to be standing alone when the guillotine falls."

"Gallows humor. I like it." Poe smiled.

"It's not meant to be funny. This is serious."

"El, have you forgotten who I am? Mr. Serious? I realize how bad this may look at present, but you have to relax."

"The manager of the Grady is involved?" Rita asked.

"He just seemed to be snooping around a lot. He mentioned the woman was in the dead man's room and that they argued. He might have heard about the jewels and decided to find out on his own. I'm sure he owns a knife or two. I still remember how ready he was to slug someone with his baseball bat. There's a lot of stored rage there." The more I talked about him, the more I could see him murdering someone.

"Sorry to douse your hopes, but he does have an alibi. The lady at the front desk can vouch for him. Seems they were, ah, busy during the time of death."

"She could easily be lying for him," I said.

"Passed a polygraph. Anyway, I can't see a motive for her lying. She doesn't need the job, and she's married, so if anything, it puts her in hot water to admit being with him. If she was going to lie, she'd say she was not with him."

"What about the knife? Were there any prints?"

"Wiped clean. Lots of prints everywhere, but it was a well-used room."

"Whoa! Whoa!" Rita interrupted, waving her arms. "Journalist here! Do I have the story? It would make a great connector to last year."

"Let's see what we can find out before you go to print," Poe said.

"And can you leave my name out? I've gotten enough attention as it is." I didn't relish any more newspaper coverage.

"We'll see what my two editors can work out. Let me know when it's set to go." Rita was in her glory, rubbing her hands together at the idea of another barnburner.

"Can you also keep dungeons out of it?"

"Are you kidding? Who needs dungeons when I have jewels, family intrigue, and maybe solving a string of robberies spanning decades."

"Speaking of families, El," Poe said. "Have you heard anything about your DNA test? Were there any family connections?"

I snapped my fingers. "I keep forgetting to do that."

"Forgetting or afraid?" Poe rubbed my arm.

"I guess a little of both," I answered.

"What will a DNA test show?" Rita asked. I could see things being added to her story.

"If any of my real family have had their DNA tested, the site will show a possible match. It would be a big clue. A doorway I'm not sure I want to walk through."

"No risk, no reward." Rita popped up. "That's become my motto. Look at me, jumping off the cliff and going to New York. I didn't know anyone. It was fail or fly."

"And you flew very well." I smiled. "I'm not sure I can do the same."

"You have to try to find out. I'm siding with the handsome Chief of Police here. Do it." She jumped up from the table and turned toward Poe. "Let's do it right now. Are you with me? Should we escort her to her computer and stand guard?"

Poe laughed. "Now that sounds like a grand idea, lovely journalist." He stood up as well. "Do I need to get my gun?"

That got Rita giggling and soon carried us with her. I sighed and rose from the table. "Okay, jump it is."

They walked me to the computer. I looked over some of the kits. "This one seems to be the most popular with the highest ratings," I said. I put in all the necessary information and hit send. "Done. Happy now?"

"Ecstatic!" Rita proclaimed. "You made the first step. Proud of you. What happens next?"

"Well, they send me a kit. I spit in a tube or take a mouth swab, send it off, and wait for results."

"Sounds easy enough."

"It is. And it's the first thing I tell clients to do when they are researching their family trees. If lost relatives are on there, they will find you."

"Well, now it's turned creepy to me," Rita said. "What if you don't want to know them? Can they like stalk you or anything?"

"From what I know, you have the option of putting your name in their database. If someone is interested, you also have the choice of responding or not."

"I like it. Will you keep me in the loop when you hear?"

"Of course. I don't text often, and I usually save email for clients, but I think we should definitely talk more on the phone."

"Agreed. Maybe when this is over, you can come visit me. I have plenty of room to put you up." She looked back and forth at us. "Both of you even." She started grinning again, and I knew something was up. "New York might even make a grand honeymoon destination."

"I think we have Hawaii for that," I spoke out of turn

before realizing what I had said. "I mean that Hawaii is also in our plans. I mean, not for any honeymoon or anything. I mean just for a place to visit."

Which sent everyone into fits. I recovered enough to say, "I mean we should take our coffee into the living room."

We moved our coffee to the new couch, which got Rita's approval again, and spent a glorious night chatting about everything and nothing at all. Too soon it was over, and Poe offered to drive Rita back to the hotel.

"Where are you staying?" I asked.

"Why, the Shady Grady, of course, Where else can a poor journalist find a good story?" She winked.

"That will be the day." I couldn't help but laugh. Some things about Rita would never change.

Chapter 11

It wasn't until later, after the dishes were done and put away and the room tidied, that I noticed Poe had left his hat behind. That was a first. Had he done it on purpose, so he had a reason to come back? My heart leapt up to a million beats imaging that was true. I had no idea where this relationship was going; I only knew it felt right, right in my brain and my heart.

I waited around for a bit, then admitted my fantasy was just that. He had left the hat behind by accident, and I was a daydreaming fool. I was just about to turn in when I heard the knock. Thinking it was him, I flung the door open without checking. "I thought you might be back."

Immediately a hand pushed me hard into the room. "Alone at last," she said, and I stared into the face of the fat dowdy woman who had been vacuuming the hallway, the one who said she didn't speak English. She held a thin sharp knife in her hand.

"Who are you? What do you want?"

"You know who I am, El. I'm the woman who is going to take possession of the diamonds."

The minute she spouted that word, Albie began chanting the numbers. It startled her for a moment, but she kept the knife pointed at my chest.

"I think those numbers is what will take us to that treasure." She saw my face. "That is unless you've found them already. That would be much easier for me. Less messy too. I tried to follow you the other day, but you gave me the slip. Getting smart now, are we? I guess you must have learned a few tricks from Lizzie."

"Who are you really" I asked. "Were you working with my mother, with Lizzie?"

"I think we both know the answer to that." She stood framed in the doorway, menacing and determined. "Now do you want to talk of your own will or does my knife need to encourage you?"

As she reached behind her to close the door, it slammed forward into her, sending her and me stumbling into the room, Poe not far behind. In an instant he put a foot on her arm as she lay sprawled on the floor and pulled out his gun. He kicked the knife away. I lay in a crumpled ball close enough to see her startled face.

"Murder! Murder! Murder!" Albie began shouting at the top of his lungs, only adding to the commotion.

"It's okay, Albie." I limped up from the floor, moved toward the cage, and tried to soothe him.

"And I think we know who you really are." Poe pulled the woman to her feet, taking a pair of handcuffs from his jacket and putting them on her wrists. "For some reason, her arms feel too soft. Maybe padded? El, I have a feeling when I take her to the station and a policewoman frisks her, we will take off the costume and disguise and find the real her. I do believe this is the partner your mother worked with. Can you grab a bag and wrap it around the knife without touching it?"

"How did you know to come back?" I asked, stunned, heading for the kitchen and doing as he asked.

"I didn't. I was headed home when I realized my head was cold and I had left my hat behind. I've never done that before." He chuckled seeing my look. "But seriously," the frown returned, "locks only work if you use them, and peepholes and chains have a specific purpose."

"Oh! Hey, will you look at that. Are you all rehearsing for a play here? Crazy." Dolly stood at the open door, her roller suitcase next to her.

Poe spun around to see who it was, the gun in his hand, and aimed at Dolly.

She put her hands in the air, a shocked look on her face. "Wow! Don't shoot, man! Is that a real gun? I thought you were practicing a play. My aunt said you lived an exciting life, El, but I didn't know it was like this."

"It's my new neighbor," I managed to get out. I motioned for Poe to lower the gun. "This is Dolly. Dolly, this is Chief of Police Alan Poe."

Poe nodded in her direction then tucked the gun in his waistband. The steel was back in his blue eyes. "Now will someone please hand me my hat."

The absurdity of it all struck me like a bolt of lightning, and I collapsed on the sofa in a fit of giggles. My emotions had finally gotten the best of me, and I sank under their weight.

Dolly spotted the hat on the rack, picked it up, walked over to Poe and set it gingerly on his head. It tilted to the side. For some reason, that act set me off again. Poe jammed the hat onto his head, steered the cleaning woman into the hall, leaving Dolly with her mouth open.

"Ah, maybe I better leave," she said. "Will you be okay?"

Holding my stomach and continuing to laugh, I

waved her off with the other hand.

"I'll just shut the door. Maybe you should lock it as well."

That set me off even more.

"Lock the door," Albie screeched. "Lock the door."

When I could laugh no more, I got up and locked the door.

****

Rita was hanging around the apartment, just like old times. She paced, she flopped on the sofa, she made coffee, she twittered around Albie's cage with a treat. The old Rita, however, would have been staring into the mirror, slathering on layers of lipstick, fluffing up a riot of hair, adjusting a too-short skirt or overly tight blouse.

"The perfect way to spend my last day in Parkville," she had proclaimed.

I was glad for the company, both of us lazing on the couch. It was an enticing blend of the old memories and the new drama.

"I heard there was a bit of excitement after I left last night. I remember something about the sins of the father, but, girl, your mother sure left a mess of them at your door."

"You think?" I said, shivering.

"Why did that woman wait until we left? Didn't she know I needed a good juicy story for my next byline?" Rita pretended to be annoyed.

"I guess some people are just rude that way."

"Spill. The whole story." She held up her hands to show she didn't have a pencil or notepad.

And spill I did. The lonely childhood that began it all, the lack of friends, the fear of who I really was, it all came pouring out like an exploding dam. In a reversal of roles, Rita listened to my ranting. Somewhere along the way, she had taken my hands in hers.

"As soon as I was old enough, my mother started sending me to boarding schools, church camps, science camps, YMCA summer sessions, anywhere to get me out of her space. We moved so often, I never got close to anyone, which I think she liked. Afraid I might let some fact or other slip inadvertently.

"When I was about 14, she farmed me out to a woman she called Aunt Ethyl for a few years. She told me Aunt Ethyl would take care of me and that my mother needed to do a great deal of traveling for her job. All I had to do was help with little chores like dusting and laundry and meals. Aunt Ethyl was really a nice old woman who didn't require much. She spent her days knitting or crocheting or sewing on quilts or baby clothes. She had closets full of things she had made. She had a small television, so I read or watched TV. I was glad to help her. She wore the same clothes for several days, so she didn't make a large amount of laundry, and she lived on canned soup, so cooking was fairly easy."

"El!" Rita shrieked. "Sorry. There's the canned soup connection."

"Oh, Rita. I never thought about it until you just pointed it out. How could I have missed that? It got to be a habit I guess I kept with me. She was more of a diehard than I was. You should have seen her pantry. Soup enough to take her through the zombie apocalypse and beyond. A million different varieties. She had more delivered to her door every few weeks. I guess it was a standing order. She was terrified she might run out." I sat back. "I'm supposed to be this observant researcher, and yet I seem to miss the most obvious things."

"Sorry to interrupt like that, but it was like a wakeup moment."

"I guess I missed that because I never told anyone about her. It's all been buried. I never told anyone about any of this."

"I'm glad you told me, El." Rita reached out and gave me a hug. "So, your mother just left you with your aunt?"

"My mother always told me she was an insurance adjuster. That's why we had to move so often and why she had to travel."

"At least you were with family."

"Another lie. I found out we weren't even related. Aunt Ethyl's daughter called when I had been there a few weeks. She asked who I was, and I told her I was Ethyl's niece. That's when she explained the world to me. She was nice about it but concerned. Since she lived across the country, she said she was going to call a neighbor just to check on us and confirm that all was well. She thought an older woman was watching her mother."

"Sounds careful. I might have done the same thing. Had you been calling the woman Aunt Ethyl?"

"Mostly at the beginning. When I found out we weren't related, I called her Ms. Vance. And she called me Lucy no matter how many times I corrected her."

"What was that about?"

"I asked her daughter the next time she called. It turned out that Lucy was the name of the woman who had cared for her before I arrived. She seemed to be just a forgetful woman, but I realize now it was developing into something more extreme. Something a young girl should not have to deal with. There I was with a woman, no relation to me, and no one else to turn to."

"Were you in contact with your mother during this time?"

"Birthday and Christmas cards. That's all. A bit of money in each envelope. I had no idea how to reach her."

"Wow, you lived a few years with a woman who you thought was family, only to find out she wasn't any relation. That's strange."

"It only gets worse. I remember when my mother first took me there; I saw her and Aunt… Ms. Vance exchanging money. I thought my mother was giving her money for my room and board. It turns out that Ms. Vance was paying her for my help. I was a live-in maid. Do you believe that? I felt like I had been sold."

"What happened? Did you mother eventually come and get you?"

"Eventually Ms. Vance's daughter told me they were putting her in a nursing home. One day my mother just showed up. They must have had some way to get a hold of her I didn't know about. She never gave me an address or phone."

"Did you move in with your mother after that?"

"Wrong. She took me to meet a casting director for a TV show—*Who Lived in Your House?*"

"I remember that show. You were on that?"

"Not on. Working for. They hired me as the assistant to the researcher. My mother lied and told them I was over eighteen. A bunch of the crew lived in this big house the show rented. I got a room, and a job, and I never saw my mother again. At least not until she called me to come to Parkville."

"What a life. This could be a movie." Rita looked my way, suddenly afraid she might have offended me. "Tell me what it was like working on the television show. Did you get to meet celebrities?"

"Not really. I was in the background of the background. A gofer. But at least I was getting paid. My own money. It felt really good. I had more or less been on my own for most of my life, so it was no big deal."

"I'm sorry about the situation. I can't begin to imagine how you must have felt. Was this any better than Ethyl's house? At least you oversaw your own life, your own money. It does sound like a wild place to live though."

"Well, the noise level was different. The crew were all older than I was. Several of the women were nice. Most of them didn't know or care that I existed. It was an almost twenty-four-hour party. I had a room in the back and stayed there with the door locked.

"During the day I worked for a woman who did the main research on the houses. If you remember, people who thought their houses were haunted or possessed could apply to the show. The researcher traveled to each city and went through deeds, newspapers, documents to see if there was any link or truth or it was just imagination on their part. She would fax me details or have me research things on her computer. I got good at it. Then the host would reveal the findings to the people on air. After a few years, my boss moved on, and they offered me the job. I was still young, but I liked the travel on company expense accounts, the eating out, the hotels. I even had an assistant. It was lonely though."

"Were some of those houses actually haunted?"

"I'm not sure we ever went that far as to use that word. Usually, we would reveal that someone had died in the house or been killed or something."

"That's spooky enough."

"Most of the time there was no substance to their suspicions. Often people would just flip out at that news. They were certain their houses were haunted and didn't want to hear the truth. They'd yell and threaten and throw things. I didn't understand that part, but they said it made for good ratings. I do remember one newlywed couple who moved into what they thought was their dream home. The first thing that happened was they began to smell odors like vanilla and cinnamon. Or like bread baking. Then they started to hear pans clanking in the middle of the night in their kitchen. When they went down, no one was there, but the smells of baking always lingered. I found records that showed a house on that spot had burned down in the 1800s with a family of six inside. All had been killed. The lot sat empty for a long time. No one wanted to touch it. Some company eventually bought the lot, demolished the ruins, and built a different home. When the couple moved in, surprise! Complete with ghosts."

"How could they live there? I would have run out screaming."

"They pretty much did. When they got the findings, they declared right there on the show that they were not setting foot in the house again. Once the show aired, they got so many offers, they created a bidding war. I think they finally sold it for a few million."

"Dollars?" Rita asked.

"Yes, dollars. I guess there's a call for true haunted houses."

"They can keep them."

I turned to Rita. "I'm sorry, but I'm spent. Rita, I'm so sorry to go on like this. It's so unlike me. I have always held my emotions close to my heart, but this past year, they have been like naughty children running wild."

"Well, all that needed to come out, and I'm glad I was here to offer the shoulder." She got up and went to the kitchen and came back with a glass of water. "I'd say this is where we need a shot of something, but if I remember right, you aren't a drinker, are you?"

I hiccupped and gave a thin smile. "Thank you for listening. I think I'm done now."

"El, I love you no matter what has happened in your life. You are you, and you are beautiful." Her eyes held a wicked glint I knew too well. "However, now that your life is out in the open, on to other important matters. I truly believe that next you need a big lounging chair," she said, pointing to a corner. "Right over there. Maybe a neon pink plaid print. And I think purple blinds rather than curtains, don't you? And possibly a bright yellow paisley wall hanging."

Soon she had me back on track and smiling.

"What's your apartment like in New York?" I asked, eager to let her do the talking for a bit.

"It's a loft. Modern. Harry owns it and lets me rent it for a fair rate." She put down her coffee and turned toward me. "So, have we approached the big subject yet? Will you expound on that topic as well?"

"Expound?" I looked at her.

"Journalists do have to widen their vocabularies you know. And don't change the subject,"

"And what might that be?" It was just like old times except she talked less about herself. Her mind seemed to be full of reporter questions.

"Marriage, silly." She cocked her head.

"Nowhere near that," I said. Too much was

happening, and I wasn't ready to bare my heart yet about Poe.

"Nonsense. I've seen the way you two look at each other. It's not far off. Remember to make me the maid of honor. And no ugly bridesmaid dresses. I want something low and sexy. Maybe black."

She had me laughing again and soon she joined in. We began to hold our stomachs as the giggles kicked in. It seemed like I was picking up where I left off the night before. We were on our way toward calling 911 for sore stomachs when someone knocked on the door. I checked the peephole but kept the chain on as I opened the door. "Yes? Who is it?"

"It's your neighbor, Dolly. Is it safe to come in? Are you all right?"

I took off the chain and opened the door wider. "Hi Dolly. Welcome back. I didn't get to say that last night. Sorry. All is well."

"Trouble, El?" Rita asked, coming up behind me.

"No. Ah, Rita, meet Dolly, the woman who now lives in your apartment and is a stand-up comedian." Turning to Dolly, I gestured behind me. "Dolly, this is Rita, who now lives in New York and works for a large newspaper."

"Hi!" Dolly put out an eager hand to shake with Rita. "You haven't come to take back your apartment, have you?"

Rita laughed. "No. I'm just visiting. Keeping El out of trouble."

"Well, you should have been here last night. What a sight. I thought I had walked into the middle of a movie set. There was a gun and handcuffs and a suspect and a policeman." She shook her head as if she still didn't believe it.

"Yes, I've been on a few of El's movie sets. They are exciting." Rita punched me softly in the arm.

"Please don't start," I exclaimed. "Sorry, Dolly. It's been an unbelievable year, and one I'd rather forget."

"Yeah, baby, I saw some of the headlines." Dolly's face broke out into the smile I remembered when I first met her. It seemed to cover half her face. "Well, it looks like you two are none the worse for wear, as they say. You survived."

"We are survivors," Rita chimed in. She put her arm around my shoulders. "Dolly, would you believe that El once lived a quiet, dull life? That the most exciting things in her life were facts and dusty old records?"

Dolly's smile stayed in place, but her eyebrows scrunched up in questions as she looked back and forth between Rita and me, trying to gauge if Rita was making a joke.

"Just a bit of New York humor," Rita said.

"New York, huh? I've always dreamed of making it in the Big Apple."

"I've heard it's a hard business to break into. Where have you been performing?"

"Any place that will have me. I hang with a bunch of other comics. We travel together to shows." Suddenly, Dolly surged forward toward Albie's cage. She had a habit of making sudden movements. "Oh! What a lovely bird."

Startled, Albie went into his *Murder! Murder!* routine.

"Easy, Albie. It's okay. Dolly, Albie has had a scare or two lately, so he's a bit touchy."

"You mean the bird gets involved in your exciting

movies?"

"Sometimes." I didn't feel like going into Albie's history at that point.

"It's probably me that scared him this time. One of the chickies I travel with takes her cat with us. I'm sure I smell like the cat."

"Birds can smell?" Rita asked.

"Absolutely," Dolly answered.

"Well, it seems I learn something new about Albie every day." I turned toward the cage. "I know he likes treats. Would you like to hand him one, Dolly?"

"Treat!" Albie recognized the word.

"Maybe next time. I still need to get unpacked and say a proper hello to Spike and Agnes. I just wanted to check that you were okay."

"Would you like your key back?" I asked.

"Keep it for now." Dolly yawned. "Besides having a man aim a gun at me, I was post-comic-trek drained last night, so I think I need about twenty more solid hours of sleep. See you all later. Nice meeting my former apartment spirit, Rita."

"You too, Dolly. If you ever decide to hit New York, let me know. My boss has leads all over the city. He might have club connections."

"Great. If you're around tomorrow, I can get your digits."

"Leaving later today, but El knows my digits."

"Yikes, she's a live wire," Rita said after Dolly had left and I relocked the door.

"That apartment has a history of live wires," I said. "I forgot to mention that she happened to come home last night, saw my door was open, and witnessed Poe handcuffing whoever that cleaning woman turns out to be. I don't recall what she said. Anyway, I turned into some kind of maniac and could not stop laughing. What has my life become?"

"El, you really need to keep a bottle of brandy around for moments like this. Jenny's tea doesn't quite go the distance."

"On my list." I pretended to write on the air with my fingers.

We settled back into our routine again, talking about her flight, people she had met in New York, anything but the recent events. Once more someone knocked at the door.

"Don't tell me Dolly is back," I said, keeping the door locked. "Who is it?"

"For me you use safety precautions?" Poe chuckled. When I opened the door, I could see the tiredness in his eyes.

"So now is it finally over?" I sighed as I took his hat.

"Pretty much. Once the policewoman helped her off with the disguise, we put her in the cell. She seemed ready to give up."

"What will happen to her?"

"She has a few decades of robberies to account for, not to mention being a murder suspect and a charge of assault with a deadly weapon on you. Depends on how much help she wants to be. Speaking of which," Poe said, "she wants to talk to you."

"What? Why me?"

"She wouldn't say, but we can both guess. Just that she wants a private one-on-one with you before she gets sent away. I got you an hour tomorrow. No cameras or recording devices. Are you interested? Besides, you have to come down to the station anyway if you want to press charges against her."

"You might get all those answers you want," Rita prodded.

"Yes, that's what I'm afraid of."

"Come on, girl, take a risk. Look what it did for me!"

Poe took my arm. "It's been leading to this. Time to make the leap."

"Fly, girl! Fly!" Rita chanted.

"Fly! Fly!" Albie joined in. It eased the tension, but only barely.

****

Email to El Turner

Ms. Turner—

Just wanted to update you on the discovery of my aunt Wilma Stone. I contacted the convent with the information you gave me. They were so nice. We were able to visit the place and see my aunt's grave. (She is buried on the church grounds.) It seems she finally found her peace there with God. The sisters do a lot of charitable work with the community, and it is a beautiful area. I am so happy she found her place in the world.

Best,

Hannah B.

Chapter 12

I debated my decision all night. Albie must have felt my nerves, for he shrieked *Murder! Murder!* off and on, even though his cage was covered. Come morning I saw that both Poe and Rita had left encouraging voice messages. Even Jenny knocked on my door to see if I needed a ride. I showered, grabbed my keys, and headed for the door before I could back out.

If there was a picture in the dictionary next to the word "spry" it would be her. The hair was gray, the face had wrinkles, but the body was taut with energy. I could see that from the door. She turned as I entered the interrogation room. On the edge of her seat, she looked ready to spring. Hands eager to move even though they were handcuffed to the chair.

"They told me the sound and video were turned off," she said, nodding me toward a seat.

"Yes, I'm sure they did." I sat, waiting to hear what she had to say.

"I'm Finn," she said. "I don't know what they have on the arrest warrant, but please call me Finn."

I must have looked confused. "Okay. I'm El."

"I know you, honey. I'd know you from a mile away." She peered at me. "I knew you the minute I bumped into you in the hallway at that hotel." She saw my look. "And before you say anything, no, I did not kill Mick. That was his brother."

"Yes, the police have arrested him, but he says he didn't do it."

"Really?" She searched my face. "Do they believe him?"

"I don't know. You were the one with the knife; he used a gun."

"Yeah, there's that. Guess they'll have to prove that one a bit better than that." She gave a knowing laugh. "I'm going away for a long time, what does murder matter in the scheme of things? Anyway, that bastard deserved it." She slammed her fists against the chair, rattling the handcuffs.

It startled me. I wondered what would happen if she tried to come at me. Would Poe know I was in trouble? I took a minute. The chair looked bolted to the floor, so I relaxed an eye blink. "So, are you saying you killed him?"

"I'm saying nothing of the sort." She looked me over carefully. "You aren't wearing a wire, are you?"

"A wire?" I was still so rattled to be there, not much was getting through my brain.

"Are you recording this? What I say?"

"Oh, no. No wire."

"I trust you."

"Why did you say he deserved to be killed if you didn't kill him?"

"Listen, I loved Mick. I mean, really loved. And I thought he loved me, but it was your mother who lured him on. He lost his mind over her. Would do anything for her. After that article came out calling us Diamond Dixies, he proclaimed her to be the original Diamond Dixie. Called her that all the time. Sometimes just DD. Bought anything she wanted. She didn't love him, but she led him along like a little puppy dog. She'd get him to take big risks for her. I never said anything because we had such a good thing going, but I hated him for it. He couldn't see that she was using him. It changed our whole dynamic and broke my heart.

"But she was setting us all up. We planned so hard for this big job. We were all in a massive con with this guy, Mick and I staying behind like we had been duped by Lizzie as well. When we finally got to the meeting place to divide the shares, we found she had left with the diamonds. At first, I thought there was some snag, but as time went by, I couldn't believe she had taken us. After all we had been through. She was like a sister to me. You don't do that to family.

"It killed Mick though. He thought they were going to live happily ever after. I was furious with her. I never dreamed she could stiff us like that. I thought then that Mick might come to his senses, come around to being with me. I would have taken him, even knowing it was on the rebound. I was that in love with the guy. Instead, he turned to the bottle, crying about his lost Diamond Dixie. He began to look like a damn alley cat. Didn't care for anything in the world. I'd check on him. Make sure he ate. I'd have done anything for him, but he could have cared less for me. Never saw a man slide down so fast.

"I searched for Lizzie for years, but she was slick. When I got word of her passing and her whereabouts, I told Mick. I thought then he might realize how she had done us bad, but when I saw his reaction, that sliver of hope in his eyes, I knew he would never be mine. She would always be his obsession. With the news, however, he revived some of the man he used to be and came looking. He thought she might have planted the obit to throw us off the track. He was ecstatic she was alive, and they could finally be together. He didn't care about the diamonds; I did."

"So you both came after her, but for different reasons?"

"Was he still alive when you went in? Did he say anything? At the end? I saw him at the hotel, just lying there, but I ran out. I didn't want to see him like that."

What tangled feelings the three of them had: She loved him; he loved my mother; my mother loved the diamonds. From what Finn had said, I realized Mick's last words had been for my mother. I just shook my head. "He was dead when I got there—"

"What about the diamonds?" she interrupted, moving on. "Where are they?"

"Found."

"Ah." She sat back in her chair as if a great weight had come off her shoulders. "Half of them were mine. Not counting Mick's share, but I guess that's mine as well. With your mother gone, they should all be mine."

"Well, I think, technically, they belong to wherever they came from." I didn't want to say stolen.

"I'm sure their insurance covered that a long time ago. I earned them."

When I shrugged, she continued. "I see you didn't come for diamond ownership, did you? Tell me about yourself. What do you do?"

"I'm a genealogist. I research family trees, documents, etc."

"It fits. You always did like reading and solving puzzles in your room."

"Do you remember when?" I didn't know how to approach the subject, but we only had a short time. Now that I was here, I had to know the truth.

"When Lizzie—how shall I say it? When Lizzie acquired you?"

I could only stare at her, dreading the answer and what was to come.

"I've been thinking about what to tell you after all this time. You know, I could spin a fairy tale. Would that make you feel better?

When I shook my head, she continued, "Let me explain a bit about Lizzie and what we did. See it all started by accident. Lizzie was in a jewelry store looking at a diamond bracelet she couldn't afford—she loved her diamonds even back then—and the clerk was called away, so she just walked out with it. Nothing happened. No police. No jewelry store came calling. And she had a diamond bracelet. She told me about it. It seemed like a lark. We were both so young at the time. We drove to a bigger city nearby. Dressed up like fancy women. Lots of makeup. Our hair styled just so. She was looking at diamond rings, and I created a diversion with the young man behind the counter, started shamelessly flirting with him. I gave him a fake number, and she walked out with a handful of gems. We took them home. I knew Mick slightly at the time; he was a low-grade fence. He got rid of them that night, and we had the money. Easy as snapping your fingers.

"And that's how it began. We did a few more runs to other cities. I had an old van we used. Lizzie always wanted to be an actress. Idolized those Hollywood women. She loved the tight sweaters and wavy blonde hair. She even suggested we write our own scenarios. We got wigs, hats, constantly changed our appearance. We had a thousand disguises. Sometimes we used modeling clay and broadened our noses or puffed out our cheeks under the makeup. Later, we even used a wheelchair. She was the nurse, and I was the patient. We traveled all over the country doing that. It was long before cell phones and the internet. Police had a sketchy database, but we never looked the same twice, so they had a hard time connecting the dots. A few times Lizzie dressed up like a man. We'd be a couple looking at diamond engagement rings. She'd pretend to get mad and storm out; I'd cry. The clerk would go get water and a tissue, and I'd make off with the goods, fleeing the store, tears gone like the wind. We could change our appearance in an instant. If there was one thing Lizzie was good at, it was planning every detail, every move, every escape.

"She kept specific notebooks of all the cities and the places we had hit as well as the dates, so we wouldn't be in the same state or city or dress the same way. Usually, we'd case a store. We'd see who was vulnerable. Who was manning the store alone. What times were the busiest and when it was slow. Then she would make all these drawings of where we should be. It was like a dance. Or a play. You stand here, and I'll walk over there. She made sure of exits and where we would go when we left the places. Made sure our vehicle wasn't too obvious or that we never drove over the speed limit or did anything to draw police attention. A time or two, we'd lift a car, use it for the getaway, then drop it. We always wore gloves. We got so we could make our getaways quick and easy. The walk was not too fast, not too lazy. Never looked suspicious. She had us practice over and over.

"Lizzie was into all sorts of schemes. For a few years, we also passed off coins that a man she knew minted down in his basement. We got a coin rolling machine and filled up tons of those coin wrappers. Then we'd go into banks and change them out for bills. She'd pretend to be an old woman who had saved up her coins for ages and was turning them into cash to give to all her grandchildren. We'd crack up over how she could change her voice to sound like all different sorts of people. She could even put on accents. After a while, we felt we needed something else. Jewelry stores were getting edgy, at least the larger ones. A lot started installing video cameras. We got to know where they were and how to turn just so to avoid them, but it was an added risk. Hats and scarves always worked well.

"That's where you came in."

I think she heard me swallow hard, but she smiled nicely like a mother telling a story to a child.

"It was fate, really. We were sitting at a picnic table at a rest stop going over a country map, choosing our next targets, discussing how to change things up. We didn't want to do too many in a row. We hit small and large cities. The big ones yielded the best prizes, but the small-town ones were so much easier to escape. And Mick was always there to fence what we brought him. We were riding a high for years. Of course, Mick blew all his money. Nice hotels. Grand meals. The best of everything.

"Anyway, we were at this park, and you wandered over. We didn't know it at the time. We had the doors of our van open to air out our sleeping bags. Back then, we often slept in the van to save money on longer treks. We got used to traveling light. We got distracted and never saw you climb into the back. You snuggled down between the bags and fell asleep. You couldn't have been more than two or three. Several cops were patrolling an area, and there seemed to be a commotion on the other side of the green, so we just closed the doors, jumped into the van, and took off. We were always on edge when the police were involved. I guess they were looking for you. We never knew you were there until you woke up several states later. We heard this whimpering in the back. Scared the sh—wits out of us. Hungry, I guess. We fed you some crackers and juice and wondered what in the world to do.

"We couldn't rightly remember exactly where we had stopped to look at the map. And if we went back, the police would be asking us questions. We didn't want the attention. If we dropped you off at a police station somewhere, there would also be questions. Same with a hospital. Someone could see us and maybe remember our van. The last thing we wanted was heat. We had been flying under the radar for so long. The Amber Alert had not been invented yet, so we were stuck.

"You finished your juice and crackers and then smiled at us. It was the biggest smile I had ever seen. You crawled into Lizzie's lap, grabbed her hand, and fell back asleep. 'This might just work out,' Lizzie had said. I remember the expression on her face. She held you in her arms and looked so happy. I had no idea what she was thinking. When she told me what she had in mind, I thought she was crazy, but she talked me into it. We didn't have many options. As soon as we could, we got the van painted, just in case someone had seen us leave. Then we cut your long hair, put you in boy's clothes, and gave you a boy's name. Anyone looking for that little girl wouldn't think twice about you. We drove halfway across the country. Mick also dealt in forged papers, so we got some for you. He got us different license plates. We couldn't keep you as a boy for too long. We called you Lane. It was easy to change it to Lana later."

"How did I fit into the robbery picture?"

"Well, we bought a stroller. The first time we tried it out, by chance you got sick all over the floor of the store. I'm still not sure if Lizzie fed you too much candy—she denied it, of course—or it just happened. But the clerk ran off to get a rag or a mop, and Lizzie took all that was on the counter. She then rushed out shouting she had to take you to the hospital. The clerk was more concerned about cleaning up the place to notice. Sometimes she gave you a lot of juice, and then took you into a store. Well, you can imagine what happened." I was horrified. Once she got going, I felt like she was confessing. Almost as if she was justifying their lives. It was an accident I couldn't avoid seeing.

"Lizzie was running the show, and there was no stopping her. I didn't mind; I had more money than I'd ever seen, and she was the one taking care of you. She was thorough, a planner. She kept a journal with her own code as to place and date and what was taken. She practiced sleight of hand; she practiced slipping things into her sleeves. She sewed certain clothes with hidden pockets to make it easier to ease things into. She'd sew clothes that were easy to get into and out of for when we had to change in a hurry. We'd check out places well, go in when only one employee was at work, usually male. She could entice a man, that was for sure. She'd go from blonde, to redhead, to raven black hair. The bright lipstick and false eyelashes. She was a charmer. She also had a book about diamonds, and it was her bible. She knew everything there was to know and could size up jewelry better than some jewelers. She knew the going rate and never let Mick take advantage of us. We had a tight group, and no one met often or talked."

"You make her sound like a terrible mother. Getting me sick or letting me go to the bathroom on the floor. Why did she keep me after my use was gone? Why didn't she just drop me off somewhere and drive away?"

"I think she was afraid you would talk. If police started to ask you questions you might give a description of her or the car or where you lived."

"But we moved around so much. I can't remember half of where we lived."

"Yes, we'd rent rooms or apartments on short term. Case out the city and leave when we had to. We didn't always take you on jobs. Often Lizzie kept you awake before a job. Then we'd let you sleep in the car while we were busy in the store. It all worked out well. You seemed happy enough."

I bit my tongue holding back what I thought of their plans and how I was treated. I quickly switched to another question. "I guess she wasn't an insurance adjuster and had to be transferred to all those places for her job?"

"No. It was her cover. I hate to say this…"

"Go on, it doesn't matter to me anymore. She wasn't my real mother."

"I think deep down she had always wanted a child, often felt like she had missed out on something. She looked on your appearance as heaven sent."

"Yeah, heaven sent to steal more jewelry," I said, starting to anger.

"Look, I understand you feeling that way, but I think she loved the idea of being a mother. She could be sweet with you. She always tried to give you the best kind of home, such as it was. You were a wonderful kid. Really. So quiet and easy to please." Finn cooed her words. "But other times, she liked the whole idea more than actually being a real parent. In the end, it was the diamonds that she loved the most. When you got older, she sent you to camp or some boarding school. Often that was when we traveled abroad."

"It was a lonely life, but one I lived through."

"Yes, you turned out well. Are you happy?"

"Yes."

"I can see you still have a question in your eyes. Ask."

"Do you know who I am? My name?"

"Not a clue. We took you someplace in New Mexico."

"Where, exactly?"

"Don't remember. I was so freaked out when the police started patrolling the park, I was a hundred county lines down the road before we knew you were there. You never could tell us your name, so we just kind of brain washed you into thinking you were a boy named Lane. Then later Lana Turner."

"One more question—what is August fifth, 1989?"

She seemed taken back by the question. "That's the day," she started saying, but stopped.

"The day of acquisition?"

"Well, yes."

"So, Lizzie just used that date as my birthday?"

"Sorry."

An officer knocked on the door and then came in. "Time's up."

"Listen, your buddy there will know where I'm

being sent. Write if you think of something else. I can't imagine how hard it must have been for you. Seeing your face now and your reactions, I want to apologize. We never meant you any harm, and I am so sorry you lost your family. If I knew who they were or who you were, I'd tell you. Lizzie was my friend, almost a sister, or so I thought. That is until she ran out on us with the biggest score we ever had. I hated her in the end for what she did to us. I still don't know why she did it." She hung her head, a sad look in her eyes, her words fading to a mumble. "She got so paranoid there at the end. Maybe Mick was pressuring her for a relationship. Maybe it all just ran its course, and she saw a way to end it…

"Anyway, I am sorry. I wish there was something I could do to make it right, but I can't change the past."

I stood up. "Thank you for telling me. I'm not sure I know what to think at this point." I felt like I had walked through the door into some sort of alternate universe. My brain was a malfunctioning computer spewing out bits and pieces of a life. I left the only connection to my past sitting at that table, slumped shoulders, and staring off into space. The truth sat like a ton of concrete on my brain.

Chapter 13

I ran. Blindly. It was all too much for me to handle. I knew Poe was waiting to talk to me, but I sidestepped him and stumbled out the door to my car in the parking lot. Rita had wanted me to call her with the news, but I couldn't face anyone right now, much less communicate. I longed to just drive and drive and think about what I had learned later. Much later. My brain, however, would not stop screaming the headlines.

My childhood had been explained, but I was no closer to finding out my real family. Finn had said they had "acquired" me in New Mexico at a park near a rest stop. Had my family lived in the state or been passing through on vacation or to visit someone? I just had to digest the truths I had discovered and worry about the rest later. I knew as a researcher, I should make notes while thoughts were fresh in my mind, but the pain of putting them to paper seemed more than I could bear.

I drove mindlessly around Parkville, meandering tree-lined streets and lonely avenues, eventually circling around the outskirts of the city. Parkville was expanding in all directions with small shopping centers, filling stations, industrial buildings popping up like metal daisies. I saw a sign for a car wash. Something in my muddled mind thought that would be a good idea. I had never washed my mother's old car. It had stayed fairly clean in the garage where I parked, but today seemed the perfect time to wash off the dirt as well as clean away my ugly past. I paid for all the services—wash, wax, and inside vacuum.

"Would you like a scented vacuum? It's no extra charge. We have lilac, pine, fresh air, jasmine—"

"Jasmine," I decided. A flowery spring smell appealed to me. I would let the scent carry me away from such a draining, traumatic day. To say it might be the worst day of my life vibrated like a joyless understatement.

"Have a seat, and we will have your car out to you, bright and shiny, in no time." The attendant pointed to a waiting room with a wall of magazines and a television highlighting sports scores. The television captivated me like a lava lamp I once had. All one had to do was stare and let the display shut out the world.

Before coming to Parkville, I had worked for a television program doing research. It was a medium I was familiar with and enjoyed watching. When I moved here to care for my mother, she didn't have a TV set, and I was surprised to see I did not miss it. After her death, and moving into my apartment, I didn't see the need. My work occupied my hours. When I wanted a rest, I read through newspapers or took a walk in the park. Today, however, the TV was just the numbing device that would take me away from myself. Sports scores flashed across the screen announcing teams and players like a foreign language I was desperate to learn. I couldn't pull my eyes away from the panorama of athletic details. For the time being, I was at peace with the entrapment.

"All ready!" The man dangled my car keys in front of me, breaking the spell.

"Thank you." I went out onto the lot where a shining

sedan awaited me. A clean vehicle for a clean start. It almost made me smile.

My mood took a distinct upswing. At least, until I opened the door. Whatever scent they had used when vacuuming came as close to smelling like jasmine as cinnamon did to ammonia. It was horrid. Caught between overpowering and thoroughly nauseating, the scent swirled around the car in odorous delight. I swear I could see the atoms dancing in the light. I hoped the scent would not attach itself to me. Rolling down the windows appeared to be the best solution.

I turned right out of the car wash lot toward what seemed like a highway and drove as fast as I could without breaking the speed limit. I didn't need to be arrested today. The air gushing in through the open windows let me catch my breath. Hopefully, that would do the trick. It seemed to have lessened the stench.

I turned around and drove back, passing the shopping center again. A sign caught my attention—Oui Bake. Jenny had mentioned that place to me, a bakery that made the best French bread. I decided to stop and buy some, maybe take a few loaves to her. The parking lot was busy, people rushing in and out of the various shops. Several spaces in front of the bakery were open, so I pulled in. Once I stopped, however, the rancid odor returned. The store had huge plate glass windows in front, so I decided to leave all my doors and windows open while I was inside. I could see the car from inside in case anything should happen. I took the keys out.

The bakery door had a chimey little bell attached to announce customers. The aroma inside was delirious. After what I had endured from the jasmine of the car wash, I wanted to live there forever. A woman came out from the back. I oohed and aahed over all the pastries and breads, finally getting four loaves of the famous French bread. When I mentioned Jenny's recommendation, the lady threw up her hands. It seemed like Jenny was a favorite. She tossed in a few pastries "for the new customer." I had my arms full of the long bags and the longer bread as well as my purse and the separate square box for the pastries. I didn't want to leave the wonderful atmosphere, but I noticed several cars parking in the spaces that had been empty. One woman in particular seemed upset because my doors were open, impeding her parking.

I rushed out of the store, juggling the clumsy long loaves and the extra box, along with my bag as I hurried to get my keys out of my pocket. Dashing around the car, I bumped the doors closed with my hip or foot, bags shifting around in my arms. I dumped them on the front passenger side seat, closed the door, and went around the front of the car so the glaring woman could drive into the spot next to mine. Keys in hand, I started the car quickly and backed out. I was hoping the woman would not get out of her vehicle and yell at me. I didn't need negativity or more drama on this upside-down day.

Driving through the parking lot, I noticed the jasmine smell was back, now smelling even worse. A mix of musty and raunchy had been added. Maybe I should take it back to the car wash and get them to vacuum again but without any odor. I wondered if I would be able to drive all the way home this way. My gag reflex was on autopilot.

I was about to leave the parking lot and head back toward town when I heard heavy breathing coming from the back seat. Immediately, I ground the car to a halt, undid my seatbelt, and jumped out of the car. Who had hidden away in my back seat when I had the doors open? I swear I had watched the car the whole time, but then I remembered the pastries and how enthralled I had been with the bread. I had no weapon, but I ran around, opened the passenger door, and grabbed a loaf of bread. I had forgotten all about the pepper spray in my bag.

"Get out of the car now!" I screamed, yanking open the back door, sturdy French loaf ready to whack any violator in the back of the car. "Out!"

The floor in the back was covered with a dirty, mangy mop of hair. Two of the saddest eyes I had ever seen stared out at me. The hair quivered and shook. A dog! How had a dog crawled into the car? The stench was overpowering. And I had just had my car cleaned! Now it was filthy. Fleas and ticks could be crawling over my car at this very moment.

I tried to prod him out of the car with the end of the bread. "Out!" It did nothing. In fact, he reached out and grabbed the end of the bread and chewed it. I tried to lure him out of the car with the bread, breaking off chunks and putting them just out of reach. Soon I put a large piece on the asphalt, and the dog leaned out of the car. His back legs were still in the car. I reached across the seat and got another loaf of bread. I tore off a nice chunk some distance from the car. He finally got all the way out. I shut the back and quickly walked toward my door, eager to be away from the wretched critter. The mess on the floor would have to wait until later.

"Hey," a man yelled from across the parking lot. "You can't leave your dog here. You need to have him on a leash."

"It's not my dog," I yelled back. "He just got into

my car when I wasn't looking." It sounded flimsy even to my ears. The man stood next to his car watching me. I saw him writing down my license number. What was I supposed to do now? I didn't want to let the dog back into my car. The man was now talking to another woman, and he was pointing at me. She took out her phone and started recording me. I looked around, hoping a policeman or police car or dog catcher happened to be driving by. In desperation, I looked at the shops.

Then I saw a sliver of hope—Parkville Pet Groomers, a small shop nestled in between the others. The dog was looking expectantly at me, hunger still rabid in its eyes. I got my purse from the car, another loaf, and locked the car door. Leaving a trail of bread chunks, I slowly lured the dog toward the pet store door, dodging drivers as we went. I could leave him at the shop. Surely, they would know what to do with him. I had garnered quite an audience. More people had their phones out and were recording my disaster. I was the hit of the shopping mall. I prayed for a huge sinkhole to open and swallow up what was left of me and my dignity.

I pulled open the shop door, saving the biggest chunk to lure the dog inside. He had eyes for nothing but the bread. I quickly closed the door.

"Can I help you?" A young girl sat behind a desk.

"This isn't my dog. It jumped into my car when I wasn't looking and scared the heck out of me. I tried to get him out by breaking off bits of bread. I was ready to leave him in the parking lot, but people were yelling and recording me." I knew I was blithering, but it had been a long and trying day, and I was nowhere near sane. "Now I'm here, and here he is. Thank you so much. I appreciate anything you can do."

An older woman in a white coat appeared. "What's the problem here?"

"No problem. This isn't my dog. I can't leave him outside. I thought you would be able to take care of him or know what I should do."

"Well, we aren't an animal shelter. All we do is groom animals. Wendy," she said to the girl at the desk, "call over to the animal shelter and see what their hours are."

Wendy dialed a number and listened, then hung up. "They're closed today."

"Now we have a dilemma," the older woman said.

"Can I take him to a nearby police station?" I asked.

"I'm afraid they will just tell you to take the animal to the shelter. The best thing you can do is take him home, put up flyers, place a notice on some social media site, and wait for the owner to call you."

"But, but, but." I was sputtering now. "I can't take him home. Look at him. He's filthy. Who knows what is wrong with him. I live in a small apartment with a parrot. I just can't! Not after all I went through today. I just can't. I mean, I really can't." I leaned against the wall.

"You look familiar." The woman walked closer and looked me up and down. "The parrot. Yes, now I remember. Aren't you the woman who saved the town last year? Getting those robbers arrested and finding the money and Clark Hill's journal? I remember seeing your picture in the paper."

"Guilty," I said, gulping. I was two tears away from a nervous breakdown.

"And now she's saving animals," Wendy cried. "You're a lifesaver. OMG a real-life hero." She stood up and clapped her hands.

The older woman sensed an imminent collapse on my part and cooed, "How about if I groom the dog for free, and you sit and think about your options? Maybe something will occur to you. It's the least we can do for a hero. Please, take a seat over there. Take a nice deep breath. There. That's it. Wendy, please bring our friend here some water." She put on a pair of gloves and reached for the dog's neck, gently guiding him into the back room.

I sat down and looked out of the window. I realized my car was parked at odds with the lines in the lot. I had parked in such a hurry when I heard the back seat breathing. I didn't need a ticket. Maybe people were still filming outside. Wendy was just getting off the phone.

"I'm going to move my car closer to the building," I said.

She nodded, but I saw her come around the desk and watch me through the glass. Was she afraid I would run off as well? I guessed I had better start acting like the hero they thought I was.

She smiled when I came back in and handed me a bottle of cold water. "I didn't get your name." Her voice had a sing-song quality.

"I thought the groomer said it was on the house."

"It is, but we still need to keep some kind of records," she said, her pen poised over her ledger.

I gave her my name, address, and phone number.

"What's the dog's name?"

"I have no idea. It just wandered into my car. I'm not sure if there is a collar or a chip of some kind. From the look of him, he's probably just a nameless mutt."

"Gaby the groomer will be able to see if there's any identification once he's washed up. She's super. I need to put a name down on the form though. How about we put in a temporary name, and we can change it if one is found?"

"I have no idea what to call him. Spot? Fido?" I was flagging rapidly. I hoped I wouldn't faint.

"Oh, we can do better than that." I hated to tell her that my brain was numb after my session with Finn and the attack of the jasmine odor. I could give a hoot about a dog's name.

"All I know is I led him in here with some French bread I had bought this morning, and now the bread is gone, and it was a gift for my neighbor." I was blubbering again.

"Well, I had a French class in high school, and I think I remember the word for bread is pan." She shrugged. "Something close to that anyway. Should I put Pan down as his name?"

"Great. Pan is great. Put down Pan."

"And what breed is Pan?"

"I couldn't begin to guess. Mutt?" Why couldn't the girl just leave me alone?

"I'll put down Mixed. That sounds better."

"Whatever."

"And how long have you had Pan?"

"Ah, like five minutes."

"Okay. Almost done. Has Pan had all his shots?"

At this point I wanted nothing more than to pound my head on the counter. I had turned my phone off so I wouldn't have to talk to Poe or Rita. Maybe I should call and ask one of them to help me. Then I remembered that Rita had left and was back in New York. We had had a tearful goodbye, lots of hugs, lots of "Let's keep in touch." I didn't think I could handle Poe's pity. How did

I end up here?

I gave Wendy an "I have no idea" sigh.

"We aren't supposed to take dogs without their shots."

"Look, Wendy, you know the situation. Fill out the form however it makes you happy. Maybe Gaby the groomer can deduce that as well." I went back to sitting down before I fell. A sudden wave of helplessness and fatigue swept over me, and I tried taking deep breaths. Was this a panic attack? I knew Poe would come and rescue me if I called, but I hated to be so weak. I turned on the phone and sent him a text instead:

—I'm fine. Talk to you soon.—

I wondered if he had police cars out searching for me.

I must have nodded off because suddenly something was licking my hand. I came to with a start to see a friendly black and white dog snuffling up to me.

"Oh, what a cute dog," I started to say. Looking up, I saw Gaby and Wendy laughing. "You mean this is… this is the gnarly matted creature I brought in?"

"This is Pan the magical dog," Wendy cried. She clapped her hands again.

"I can't believe it," I said. "You have done wonders."

"A simple wash and groom. Amazingly no fleas or ticks. It looks like he may have some sheepdog in the mix. If you want to make another appointment, I can see to the details—ears, toenails, etc."

"I don't think I need another appointment. He's not my dog. I'm sure an owner will come forth."

She didn't seem to be listening. "You also need to take him to the vet for shots, etc."

I wanted to repeat he wasn't my dog, but the universe didn't seem to care. The universe wasn't listening. "Thank you so much," I said and bought the cheapest leash, collar, and dog food they had. He wouldn't be around long enough to waste the money on.

The one lonely loaf of bread left on the seat seemed to mock me as I got into the car. I took a newspaper out of the trunk and spread it on the dirty parts of the floor. Patted the back seat for the dog. He jumped in as if it was his rightful place. He looked out the window all the way home. At least he was polite.

****

Poe cracked up when I told him about it later that night. He wouldn't stop chuckling and shaking his head in disbelief. I think part of it was his immense relief I hadn't jumped off a cliff or just crashed into the sunset. I told him how Albert had stopped me on the way up and had given me a lecture, a form to fill out for pets, and a request for a deposit. "He won't be staying," I had answered. Albert went by the books and, much like the rest of the universe, didn't seem to care, so I took the forms. He did a tsk-tsk, shook his head, and sent a deep sigh my way. I tried to picture myself as a dog person. It didn't register in my mind's camera.

I hadn't considered how Albie might react. The minute we walked through the door, he began, "Murder! Murder! Murder!" That was all I needed—the rotten cherry on top of a melting nightmare sundae.

I had hustled the dog into the office bedroom, gathered a few old blankets to put on the floor for a bed, filled a bowl with water, and put some dog food on a plate. "I'm afraid you will have to stay here for tonight. I have a parrot who is crazy, and I can't deal with any of it right now." I closed the door. The minute the dog was out of sight, Albie quieted.

When Poe stopped by, his reassurance was evident. "I thought something had happened to you. Rita was going crazy with worry. I even went down and knocked on the new neighbor's apartment to see if she knew where you were. I think she's sorry she moved into this building."

"Something did happen." I opened the bedroom door where the dog was sleeping peacefully on his makeshift bed.

"El, I think Parkville is making up for all your dull, calm years." He put his arms around me in a big bear hug that would have sent my heart into overdrive on any normal day. He was a head and a hat taller, but I fit very nicely against his shoulder. "I'm all ears. Give it to me," he said.

I gave him a summary, too tired to delve into gory details.

"Fate works in weird ways." He tried to hide his smile as he turned away, but I could see his shoulders shaking.

"Please stop. I'm way too exhausted to even cry."

He sat me down, raised my feet up on the footstool, and went into the kitchen to fix me a sandwich. I knew he wanted to hear about my talk with Finn, but he sensed it better not to ask me anything more tonight.

I nodded off again after the sandwich. When I woke, I heard Poe's soothing voice in my office. When I padded in, I saw him sitting on the floor petting the dog. I had never seen such a happy look on his face before.

"What a great dog. I took him for a long walk. I hope you don't mind. I also explained to him that he must behave around Albie. I think he understands."

"He's gone as soon as I can make up some flyers tomorrow. I thought I'd send one to the bakery and the grooming place since he was in that neighborhood. Put his picture on social media."

"Hey." Poe put his finger to his lips and stood up. "Let's talk in the other room." He motioned me out of the room and closed the office door.

"What? He can't understand what I'm saying."

"He gets the tone. He's a smart dog. Loveable. You aren't giving him away, are you?"

"He's not mine! Doesn't anyone get that? He's not my dog. I don't want a dog. I don't need a dog. First a parrot drops onto me, now this dog." I stomped my foot on the floor like an angry child.

"Okay. Okay. Calm down. Ah, if you remember, that parrot you didn't want saved your life last year."

"I know, and I've finally come around to liking him and being used to him. A dog is a whole different adventure. If you forget, I live in a small apartment. I'm not even sure what the pet rules are here for dogs. I only half listened to Albert's guidelines sermon. Why don't you take him?"

"First off, I'm hardly ever home. Second, why don't we wait to see if anyone claims him?"

"I could just take him to the animal shelter tomorrow and let them deal with it. We tried to call today, but they were closed."

"Yes. They had a leak in the place. Water pipes burst. They are in the process of cleaning up the mess. They will probably be closed for a week or more."

"Oh, great. The whole world is conspiring to drive me crazy."

"Listen. I know what you need. Why don't you take a nice hot bath? Light a few candles. Take in a glass of wine." He saw my look. "Or take in the whole bottle. Unless you and Rita drank it all up. I'll watch the dog and have a talk with Albie. See if we can sort out this mess and make life bearable for a few days. I'll knock on the door in an hour, so you don't fall asleep in cold water. Then you can lock the door behind me and toddle off to bed."

"Sounds wonderful, but it's already so late. Surely you must be tired."

"I think I can handle it. I'm just so glad you're okay."

"Thank you so much for everything. You are one amazing man, Chief Poe."

The passion in my voice was clear, even to my tired ears. I pointed toward the bathroom and ran the water. My pajamas and bathrobe hung on the door hook and looked more inviting than an eighteen-layer chocolate cake. When he knocked an hour later, I was in a much better place. I put on my bedclothes and saw him to the door.

He kissed me on the cheek. "Sleep well. Remember you have a dog now, so he will have to be taken out in the morning." I nodded. "We can talk tomorrow."

As he reached for the door, I grabbed his arm, turned him around, and drew him into my arms. "I am so lucky to know you, Alan Poe. So lucky." I returned the hug he had given me earlier. I didn't want to let go.

He gave me an embarrassed aw-shucks grin and left.

"I'm waiting to hear the locks click," I heard through the door.

"Yes, sir!"
I dreamt I ran a circus, and then all was black.

Chapter 14

Somewhere a dog was barking. I tried to swat the sound away, but it only got louder. Then I remembered the creature in the next room. I lumbered out of bed, went to the office, and opened the door. A huge ball of fluff flew at me, paws on shoulders, dog breath in my face, tongue slobbering all over my cheek.

"Down! Down! Let me get dressed and we can go out." I wasn't sure I was ready for this. I was still sodden with yesterday's drama.

The dog sat and waited while I uncovered Albie. I prepared for the shrieks, but the two just eyed each other. I changed my clothes, got the leash, told Albie I would be right back, and off we went. I decided to make the trek over to Basset Park. It seemed unusual for Jenny to not stick her head out, but Poe must have told her to give me some space. I hoped he had told Dolly the same thing. I really couldn't handle her energy this morning. A dog was enough!

Somewhere in Parkville's history, a mayor had decided to reflect the city name by creating a variety of parks. He had also declared his patriotic leanings by honoring the thirty-nine signers of the constitution. Each of the men was now reflected in a patch of grass, a few trees, and a metal plaque. Washington was the first, biggest, and most accessible public area.

In time, the proud citizens of Parkville had dictated

each park's designation. Basset Park, where we were headed, quickly became a favorite of all the dog lovers in town. In an attempt to bring equality to pets everywhere, Morris Park had soon been taken over by cat people. When the local library needed a bigger building, they situated it near Read Park. Veterans and war aficionados liked to gather at Sherman Park and urged the city to situate a small tank near the benches. Clymer Park eventually turned into a tangle of jungle gyms and other playground contraptions perfect for wearing out energetic children. Mifflin Park became coupled with Mifflin Muffins, a popular bakery. People ate their baked goods across the street in the park, the delicious crumbs enticing most of the birds around.

I hoped by avoiding my usual park forays, I would not run into Mr. Marquez or Will Pepper. Both men were friends and ones I would usually dearly love to see, but this morning I wanted to be alone with my thoughts. Besides, I had never walked a dog before. I wasn't sure of the protocol or how Pan would react, but he was a respectable walker as well, not yanking on the leash or trying to drag me along at a rapid panting pace.

Despite the situation, it felt good to be out and about so early in the morning. The air was fresh and crisp. Trees were just starting to rev up their colors. Yesterday seemed like scenes from a book I had recently read or a play viewed last month. The events had little to do with me. Yet here I was, walking a dog I hadn't owned yesterday and still trying to make sense of who I was.

The trails at Basset Park were shady and still, even with all the other dogs around. I felt like I was losing myself in the shadows. Pan seemed more interested in the bushes than the other animals. I was really getting the hang of this dog business until I realized one needed to bring bags along. I patted my pockets, but there was nothing even resembling a bag. Too many people around to make a run for it. I had had my fill of people filming me with their phones.

"If you're looking for bags, check out the dispensers around the park." The man was middle aged and a scowler, but he pointed toward a handy blue dispenser.

"Thank you so much!" Relief flooded through me.

"We doggies have to stick together." He gave an unexpected smile and headed off, a low-bellied dachshund ambling along beside him. Pan barked a thank you as well. It felt good to be part of a community, even if it was with a dog I was going to give back to its owner.

The rest of the morning I faxed out flyers, searched social media, and plastered pictures of Pan in as many places as possible. Then I turned to much-neglected research work. In between a few more walks, the dog slept the day away. Albie pretended we didn't have a dog.

****

Email to Tanya Hearst

Dear Ms. Hearst:

First, let me apologize for not getting back to you sooner. I am sorry to say I could find nothing about your parents. If people want to get lost in our country, there are many ways to do it—fake documents, name changes, etc.

Second, I think I found your brother. I tried a search for Nathan Hearst in West Virginia and surrounding states and found several. On examination, most had families that were traceable. I emailed two that seemed promising and asked them if their parents had ever lived on a commune in that state. One did not reply; the other did. I am attaching a part of his response below.

"I grew up on a commune in West Virginia with a wonderful family. This commune used first names only in addressing each other. When I turned 19, I left the commune. My parents (Ocean and Twinkle) sat me down and explained that they had raised me as their own after my birth parents left me behind and told me my real last name. After they had lived there a while, my birth parents made a sudden departure. They thought I was too young to travel and asked if they could leave me in Ocean and Twinkle's care for a week or so. When my birth parents never returned, Ocean and Twinkle who raised me decided to keep my origins a secret. No one in the family or commune ever brought it up. I now have a family of my own. I was thrilled to hear I might have a birth sister. I took a DNA test after I left the commune, but never got a match for anyone. If she chooses, she can do a test herself, and we can find out for sure if we are related. If this is on the level, I would be happy to meet with her."

I would suggest you follow his advice and get a DNA kit and see if you are a match. Your imaginary friend might be real.

Please let me know how it turns out.
Best,
El Turner

****

"Any luck finding the owner?" Poe asked over the phone a few days later. An overload of cases had been keeping him busy. I wondered if he was feeling remorse or embarrassment for all the hugs we had shared and wanted to keep our distance.

"No," I wailed. "I have never taken so many walks in the park in my life! I'm going to have to get a bigger supply of baggies. It's something I never thought about the first time. Ugh! I won't forget it again. Luckily, Bassett Park isn't that far away, and they have bag stands!"

"How are you doing on dog food? Should I pick up more?"

"Does that mean you will actually be able to come to dinner tonight?" I thought of my cupboards and how bare they had become. Too much was going on. I had kept up a steady stream of inquiring emails to the bakery and the nearby shops; so far, no one had claimed or lost a dog.

"Looks like it. Why don't I pick up some dog food and some human food along the way? Then no one will have to cook."

"Wonderful idea."

"I think we may have a lead on our young thief, the one who was taking all those small random items. I'll fill you in when I see you."

I felt a cold nose on my arm. "Another walk? I swear I've lost ten pounds in just a week." I feared my quiet days would be gone forever along with any fantasies I might have had about Hawaii.

****

"All we ever got on any camera was a shot of a thin man wearing a dark green hoodie pulled around his face. No vehicle we could see. No distinguishing tattoos or scars of any kind. He seemed to be carrying a backpack like a million other kids out there." We had just finished feeding Pan and Albie and ourselves. Poe had taken Pan for a short walk while I made coffee. We settled down on the sofa, his feet up on the footstool.

"So what if he is taking little items. No big deal, right?" I asked.

"Taking something another person owns is theft."

"What if he has a good reason?"

"And what would that reason be to break the law?"

Just then his phone rang.

"Yes. Yes. I'll be right there."

"You have to go? Now?"

"We have a lead on another case. I'll call you tomorrow." He looked like he was about to say something else but ended up just nodding. He pointed at the locks.

"I know. I know."

I had hoped to tell him about my conversation with Finn, but tonight appeared not to be the time. I washed out our coffee cups and disposed of the take-out containers. Pan wandered off toward his bed. Albie nestled into his wing. Poe hadn't left his hat behind.

****

"A dog? What in the world has come over you? I know people have after-trauma reactions, but how does acquiring a dog fit in?"

"It's not my dog, Rita. That's what I keep trying to tell people."

"Okay. I could hear that sigh all the way to New York. Tell Mother Rita the whole story. I've got unlimited talk on my phone."

"Well, I won't bore you with the long version, but he jumped into my car, and now I can't find what mortal owns him."

"And what does Albie have to say about this?"

"It seems Poe is a dog whisperer as well as a bird

whisperer."

"You've got yourself a regular zoo happening there. Any cats in your future?" Rita laughed at her joke. "Sorry. I don't mean to laugh when you're upset. Hey, what about that new lady in my old apartment. Would she take the dog?"

"She's gone half the time. She can barely take care of a pair of cacti."

"Jenny?"

"Listen, it's wonderful of you to call, but can we change the subject?"

"I just wanted a follow up on your event in the police station with your mother's friend. What did you find out? I tried getting through to you, but your phone was off. I figured you didn't want to talk about it, and then my plane was due to take off, and it's been a whirlwind since I got back. So, I'm listening now. How's that for changing the subject?"

"I'm not sure I want to get into that one over the phone either. Sorry. Let's change the subject to you."

"I thought you would never ask. I'm doing a piece on the D-i-a-m-o-n-d Dixies."

"I don't think you have to spell it out over the phone, Rita. Albie isn't eavesdropping on the other line."

"Right. Well, I did some digging into them and came up with—"

"Whoa! Wait a minute. Are you telling me you have been doing research? Now it's my turn to say, what have you done with the real Rita Starr?"

"Okay. Okay. You think I spent all that time in your apartment and didn't absorb anything?" I heard her offended-sounding sniff, then the giggle.

"I'm impressed." I laughed too then had an

afterthought. "Please don't mention me."

"Yeah, I got that message. I'm doing the story on them, and it has nothing to do with you. At least not at this point. Later, if you want to join in on my headline stories, you are more than welcome."

"What's your angle?"

"My angle, my dear El, has a women's issue filter. I found that old newspaper clipping where the writer thought women weren't smart enough to plan these robberies. I'm going to prove him wrong." She paused for effect. "And you won't believe this, but the man is still alive. I contacted him about the story, and he even gave me a quote."

"Which is what?"

"He remembered it well and stands by his story. Guess he wants to go down with his misogynistic ship."

"Sounds exciting, especially the part where you leave me out."

"My editor wants me to try to contact your mother's friend. Maybe do an in-prison interview. I told him I would have to run it past you first. I don't want to step all over your life again."

"I think it's a great idea."

"You do? I was waiting for the shouted NO to come through."

"Would it be possible not to identify my mother? If you just made the story about Finn?"

"I think that could be arranged." Again, there was the pause.

"What else? I know you well enough to know when you hold something back."

"My editor also wants me to do another murder in small peaceful little Parkville. That story last year went through the roof. I've got it half written and don't need to add your name."

"But won't people start digging? Find out the connections?"

"Yes, they probably will dig. That's why I wanted to ask you first."

"Why not?" I shook my head. "After all, I have a guard dog now."

When we stopped laughing, she went on. "I also contacted our illustrious Chief Poe to see what he thought. He even agreed to help me meet up with your mother's friend and give me a quote or two. After all, since she confessed, you are no longer a person of interest. Your involvement in this mess is over."

"What? She confessed? When did this happen? Did Poe tell you that?"

"Oops. Sorry if I stepped on his punch line. With all that was going on, he probably hasn't had a chance to tell you."

"He was here the other night, but then he got called away. He's been busy as well."

"Well, don't tell him I let the dog out of the bag." She chuckled at her own joke.

"Thank you for letting me know. That's one thing I no longer have to worry about. Did Poe say what prompted her to confess?"

"Not a clue. I guess you will have to get that from him." I had been waiting for the right time to tell him about my meeting with Finn, but that time had not happened yet.

I breathed a sigh of relief and then turned back to her. "Your story sounds great. Rita, I have to say you are getting darn good at your job."

"Darn good! Darn good!" Albie began his recitation in the background.

"Man, that is one bird who cannot keep his mouth shut," Rita said.

Our reminiscing led us to a cheerful place and then it was time to hang up. "What kind of doggie treats should I pack along with Albie treats? Love you, El!" I heard the giggle.

"Love you too, Rita," I said, but the dial tone showed she had hung up. I wondered if I should change my name to avoid any attention bound to come my way. My brain, oblivious to all else, danced with the tattooed rhythm of *No longer a suspect. No longer a suspect. No longer a suspect.*

****

To stop the avalanche of thoughts about my mother and her escapades, I took Pan for another walk. It was becoming a habit I was starting to enjoy. Most of my adult life had been spent indoors in dusty records rooms and library basements. The outdoors was growing on me. Physical exercise began to replace mental aerobics. I had begun to familiarize myself with the other parks in town. Today might be a good time to visit one of the smaller, more out-of-the-way ones. People at the dog park were a bunch of regulars who liked to converse on subjects dog related, which was fine, but today I wanted new faces.

I looked at a town map and decided to make the trek over to King Park. It was a fair distance, but the weather was beautiful, and Pan seemed ready. I put a few bottles of water in my backpack. The park sat among one of the underdeveloped areas of Parkville. I saw lots of trees and shade and not a lot of people, which suited me just fine. The houses along the way were older and had larger lots.

Gardens and flowers seemed to sprout everywhere. A few rabbits even crossed our path, but Pan seemed as uninterested in them as he was in all the trees.

It wasn't until we had taken one of the footpaths that led into the park that I saw an opening ahead. The trail emptied into a large central area. There people of all sorts were playing games.

"Now I'd like to think that was a friend of mine, but as far as I know, she doesn't have a dog." I recognized the voice instantly.

"Sarge! What are you doing here? I thought you hung out at Sherman Park."

I walked over to where he and another man were playing a game of chess.

"Girlie, what you don't know about me would fill a library."

"I guess Sarge never told you he was a chess master, did he?" The other man spoke up.

"No, he never did."

"Ha! No master about it. I just tinker around with the pieces. I really come here to see where all the action is happening."

I looked around. Table after table was occupied with people of all ages, intent on the boards in front of them. Dozens of onlookers stood in silent contemplation. Even though most of the area was still, there was electricity in the air even I could feel.

"I don't mean to interrupt your game. Sorry." I felt like I should whisper.

"Just a friendly one."

"Yeah. Sarge here could play a winning game, carry on a conversation, and probably dance a jig at the same time."

"Really? You just never know, do you?" I laughed. If there was anyone I could have run into on the walk, it was Sarge.

"Who's your friend?" Sarge reached down and rubbed Pan's ears, trying to get the conversation away from him. I could almost hear Pan purring.

"Long story. He's lost. You get around, Sarge. Have you ever seen him before, maybe seen someone walking him? I've plastered this town with flyers, but so far no one has come to claim him. I think I asked every soul at the dog park."

"Don't think so. You, Billy?"

"Nope."

"Billy, I want to introduce you to the famous El Turner, champion defender of Clark Hill, and hero extraordinaire. El, meet William Shears."

"Another William? Nice to meet you."

"Sarge and I met years ago. Found out we had the same name and needed to go by something else. Found out our names connected on several layers. Sarge here was Will before he became Sarge. I became Billy. It all worked out."

"I guess you might be the source to fill me in on the life and times of Will call-me-Sarge Pepper."

Sarge almost choked. "Not on your life. Me and Billy here have secrets we hold on to for each other so you won't get far with your questions. Billy, El is a first-class researcher, so be wary when she starts asking innocent things."

"I have been visiting a lot of the parks since this dog came my way, but I didn't realize this one had a specialty."

Billy looked around. "King Park—the perfect place

to offer games with a king in chess and a king me in checkers. Plus, it's out of the way. Kids, unless they have an interest in the game, don't come here too often. Making noise is frowned upon." He pointed at Pan. "So, you better not bark." Pan put his head down on his folded arms. We all laughed.

"Well, we better be heading back. It's a long walk. I think it's done us both good. I'll say we sleep well tonight."

Before we left, I took one of my water bottles from my pack. I looked about for something to pour water in for Pan. Billy put his empty cup on the ground.

"I couldn't let him drink from your cup. You might want to use it again."

"Go ahead. I drank from much worse things in the war." He grabbed the bottle from my hand and filled the cup for Pan. His slurps emptied it in no time. "Take it with you. I got more in the car." He pointed over to a parking lot I had not noticed.

"I guess we came in the long way. Didn't realize there was a quicker way."

"Girlie, you live in this town long as we have, you'll get to know every inch of soil."

"Good luck with the game. Nice to see you again, Sarge, and nice to meet you, Billy."

"Keep your eyes open. Never know where I'll show up next." Sarge laughed.

****

Email to El Turner

Well, I've gone and done it. Maybe the wife was right when she said I couldn't do anything right! Anyway, she's giving me another chance, and I don't want to blow my chance. She said if I straighten out the bills and get them paid like I was supposed to, she will forgive me. The thing is, I don't remember who the horoscope lady is that sent me the horoscopes. I just remember she lived in the same state you do and had a picture of herself with a snake around her neck on her website. I can't find that website anywhere or any bills from her. I got the other bills taken care of, but she is the last. I looked up genealogist in the dictionary and saw where I made my mistake. Now I do need your services though. Can you find this horoscope lady for me so I can pay her bill and get my wife back? You will be saving my life and my marriage.

Paul, the future almost back with his wife husband
****

Email to Paul, the future almost back with his wife husband

Dear Paul,

I am all for second chances! I have included the information you want below. The lady you seek (astrologist) did have a picture up on her website with a feather boa around her neck. You might have seen the word boa and remembered snake. She was anxious to know if the horoscope she did for you mentioned this wrinkle in your married life. Maybe you could bring her up to speed when you pay her bill.

Happy life to you and your wife,
El Turner (genealogist)

Chapter 15

"Well, it seems I have a day off," Poe said. "Imagine that."

"It's Saturday."

"Well, it seems I have a Saturday off. Do you want me to drive you and Pan to the vet or the groomer?"

"Let's do the vet today. Shots are probably more important. It looks like I may be stuck with this creature, so it's good to keep him healthy."

"Dogs can sense your tone, you know," Poe cautioned.

"That means if I'm mad or disappointed, I should sing my words?"

"Now, be nice. Along the way home, I have a stop to make," he said as we got into his car.

"Of course. It's what you do on your days off. By the way, isn't there something you want to tell me? Something that I really need to hear for my sanity and peace of mind?"

He scrunched his eyebrows together in a questioning look. "Like what? Can you give me a hint?"

"Like me not being a person of interest anymore?"

"What? I thought I mentioned it the other night. Please tell me I mentioned it the other night."

"You might have thought you did, but no."

"I guess our little journalist brought you up to date. I'm so sorry, El. I wasn't sure you wanted to talk about

Finn, and it didn't seem right to tell you over the phone; I guess with everything that's happened with the dog and all, it slipped my mind. Sincere apologies to the lady who is no longer a person of interest. You have the official word. I have something to talk to you about, but I'll wait for a more private place."

"Oooh, that sounds mysterious. Now that I have the official word, that's one box I can check off the list. It's a tremendous relief. I know we have a lot to do today, so I will save all my questions until we have more time."

"Thank you. I really want to follow up on this lead we got. It's getting out of hand. The neighbor of an older woman saw unusual activity at the old woman's house by a boy in a dark green hoodie. She had heard rumors around the neighborhood to be on the lookout. When officers went to the older woman's house last night, she refused to talk to them or let them in. Said she didn't trust those badges. I thought maybe with you along, and in the light, she might be a little more talkative."

"And here I thought you wanted to spend time with Pan and me. Turns out we're just cover for you."

The vet wasn't busy, so we got in right away.

"This is one of the gentlest dogs I've seen in a while," the vet said as he brought Pan back out to the waiting room. "Since you don't know the history, we started with all the basics. This is one smart dog. It's almost as if he understands what's going on. I'm surprised no one has claimed him."

"I guess I have." I took the leash and led him outside. He jumped into the back seat of Poe's car and proceeded to look out the window. "I'm glad he's polite. I don't think I could handle a yippy ball of energy."

"So how do you spend your time with him?" Poe

asked.

"What do you mean? I've been taking him on tons of walks. I think we know every inch of the dog park by now. I hardly have time for anything else."

"Do you have a lot of clients at present?"

"No. I've been using the time to process all that happened. Is that allowed, Chief?

"Of course, it is. I just wondered about the time you spent with Pan. There are other parts of having a dog."

"You want me to go out and throw a ball for him too?" I wasn't sure where he was heading with this line of questioning.

"Nothing so vigorous. Not unless you want to, that is. I guess I was going more toward petting him, rubbing behind his ears, talking to him. Most dogs love to be touched and petted. It shows you care."

"Walking for miles doesn't show I care?"

"Certainly it does. I was just saying that you can pet a dog or rub his ears while you are reading a newspaper. Dogs don't care if you multitask."

I didn't answer him. I wasn't sure I had one. So far, I had been balancing the line of not getting attached. I could walk and feed the dog. Take it to the vet or groomer. Touching and patting and talking to the dog crossed that line. It invested me. It deepened the fear that someone might come out of the shadows and claim him just when I got close.

We drove to a small rundown house, leaving Pan in the car. A suspicious eye peeked out from behind a door chain. Poe explained who he was and showed his badge.

"How come you ain't in a police car? And who is that?" She pointed at me.

"That is El Turner."

"She a cop too?"

"No, ma'am. She is a genealogist. You might have read about her in the newspapers last year when she found Clark Hill's journal and saved the town."

"What if I say I will only talk to the woman?"

"Well, she can't make a proper police report; I can."

"Report about what?"

"We just have a few questions about a boy in a green sweatshirt who came to your house the other day."

"Petey? What do you want to know about him for? He's a good boy."

"Just some general questions. Would it be all right if we came in?" When she didn't budge, Poe amended, "Or we can just ask them from here."

"Ask."

"What is Petey's name?"

"Told you. It's Petey."

"Does he have a last name?"

"Never asked."

"Is he related to you? A grandson or nephew maybe?"

"No. Just a boy who visits me."

"Does he ever ask for money?"

"Knows I don't have any." She looked ready to slam the door. "Brings me things though."

"What sorts of things?"

"Brought me flowers once."

"Flowers?"

"In a pot. Flowers in a pot. Said someone had left them to die so he took 'em home and brought 'em back to life and he give 'em to me. Pretties things up a bit. Brings me magazines to read too. Gonna arrest him for that?"

"So, he bought some magazines and gave them to you."

"I said brought not bought, man. You deaf? Someone was throwing them away, he said. Perfectly good magazines. They tore the back cover off. I can't get out anymore, so he brings me things to help me pass the time. Long as my eyes hold out, I can read about the world I can't get out into."

"What else has he brought you?"

"Packets of stuff."

"Like?" Pulling teeth would have been easier.

"You know, sugar, salt, pepper. He helps a lot of people around here. Don't see anything wrong with that. You going to tell me it's against the law to help folks now?"

"Can you tell me someone else he has helped that you know about?"

"Petey sometimes takes things to Mrs. Marian next street over. I used to visit with her when I had my walking legs on."

"I think I get the picture. Let me leave my card with you. If he comes back, would you call me?"

She didn't make a move to take it. "Ain't got no phone."

"Well, thank you for your time. We appreciate it, ma'am."

"What do you make of that?" I asked when we got back in the car.

"I've got an idea." He picked up his phone. I heard him asking for an address for a Mrs. Marian. "Next stop."

Mrs. Marian was more than eager to express delight in Petey's gifts. "He brought my boys a basketball each.

Ours got punctured by these older boys, these bullies, so one day he showed up with the balls. Said he knew some people who had plenty of them and they were happy to share. He also brought over a lawn chair for my mister to sit outside. One of those long ones where you can put your legs up. He hasn't been able to work since the accident, but he loves to sit outside and listen to the birds. The concrete stoop is too cold and hard on his leg. It was a used chair, but still in fine condition. He's just always helping folks, bringing gloves and hats and socks for kids that need them."

"You wouldn't happen to know where he lives, would you?"

"I know he's a student at the college."

"Do you know his last name?"

"I think it's Peter Barrie. He told me once he had a scholarship. Such a sweet boy."

We thanked her and left.

"Are you up for one more stop?" Poe asked.

"Let me walk Pan and then we will be."

We stopped at a park and took him for a short walk.

"Are you getting the same ideas I am?" I asked.

"Yup. Those things he takes—those food packets could easily come from a restaurant or even the college cafeteria. Magazines from some office with a waiting room. He tears off the back cover so no one knows where they came from. Taking a basketball or two when there are several just lying around outside."

"Taking from the haves and giving to the have nots. Sounds familiar." I stopped on the path. "He wears a green hoodie. Kind of like a certain fellow who lived in the forest and wore green."

"It is understandable when you think about it, but

it's still against the law."

"But you can't throw someone like that into jail," I protested. We walked slowly back to the car.

"Let's see what the college has to say."

In the dean's office, we collected information about Peter Barrie: Father deceased. No mother listed. Scholarship student based on need. We were getting the picture loud and clear.

Walking over to the dorm, we heard raucous music coming from his room before we even got to the door. Poe had to hard knock several times. A wave of pot smoke slapped us in the faces when the door opened. The unkempt boy inside was holding a box of fried chicken, his lips and fingers shiny with grease.

"Bill Sadler?" Poe held out his badge.

"Oh geez!" The boy stumbled over shoes and towels on the floor trying to get to the computer to turn down the music and open the window.

"Some guy just left, officer. He was the one smoking in here. I told him it wasn't allowed, but he wouldn't listen. I had to throw him out." He proclaimed the flimsy story as truth, still holding the box in his hands.

"Really?" Poe looked him up and down, peeked around him to examine the room.

"Honest." He finally put down the box of chicken, throwing it onto one of the beds.

"Actually, we are here to see if Peter Barrie is around."

"Who?"

"Your roommate."

"Oh, is that his name? He was only here about three weeks, and then he got a job house sitting for a guy who was going to be gone for several months. He said he needed the money." He shrugged. "We didn't really match up."

"And where might this house be?"

"I think he said it was somewhere along Sherwood Avenue. Probably has a bright blue bike on the front porch. That's what he uses to get around."

Poe stared intently at the boy, who was now shifting from foot to foot uneasily. He finally nodded his head and walked away. I followed. I wondered what kind of nightmares the boy might have tonight.

"I guess you're off to chase bad guys," I repeated his phrase. "Be nice."

"I'll take you and Pan home," he said, his mind already onto other issues.

"Let me know what happens."

****

Email to El Turner

Yes! We are a match! He is my actual brother! It is unbelievable that you found him for me. We met last week and had a wonderful talk. I am going to meet his wife and children soon. I have a family now and it feels wonderful!

Thank you! Enclosing some pictures. You will certainly see the resemblance.

A grateful Tanya Hearst

****

He appeared that evening with a bag of Chinese take-out. Pan jumped up and licked his cheek.

"That's one habit I need to talk him out of," I said. "What happened with Peter Barrie? Did you arrest him?" I was hoping he would say no. "Surely there are worse criminals out there for you to chase down." All day I had wondered about the boy who helped others. What was his story? The researcher in me was antsy.

"We took his statement."

"So? Don't leave me in suspense." I got out plates and put the food on the table.

"It's complicated. He's a first-time offender. He never stole anything over a certain amount from a store. The things he stole—used magazines from several doctors' offices, packets of condiments from the student commissary, two beach towels taken from several that were drying on a porch railing and given to a homeless man to use as a blanket, two basketballs from those that were left outside at the community center court, dying plants someone forgot on a stoop that he rejuvenated, and the list goes on. None of it was for himself. All for people who needed it."

"Yes. Truth mirroring fiction."

"He's on scholarship at school, and an arrest could make him lose that. All in all, you're right, we have larger issues to use our man and woman power on. Peter Barrie's adventures were enough though to get a whole area of town in an uproar. Our phones have finally stopped their hardy ringing. I'm going to discuss it with the college dean and see if there is some way for him to work off the charge with community service. None of the people really wanted to press charges when they heard the story."

"Community service? Doing what?"

"No idea. But I see from your expression that one or two ideas burst through your atmosphere just then."

"I got an amazing letter today. It seems I'm getting a reward for the recovered jewels. I called Rita because, technically, she deserves half, but she said to use it for something worthwhile."

"Another one? Didn't you and Rita share a reward for the stolen money you both found last year?"

"Yes, and we used it to start the Parkville Historical Society. They have gotten quite a few donations since, enough to cover moving to the old Hill House and converting it into a museum. Rita's stories helped. A lot of people took notice."

"And what do you want to use this one for?"

"Can I talk to Peter Barrie? Is that possible?"

"He's not in custody. We released him on his own recognizance with the dean in agreement. There will be restrictions on him through the college, I'm sure. How about I sit in on the meeting?" He started to dig into the food. "You aren't going to tell me your ideas, are you?"

****

We met at the police station. I took Charlotte Webb along with me and introduced her to Peter. He had a thin face with an indrawn look. Eyes on the table in front of him. I could see a shock of white hair under the hoodie.

Poe sat quietly, and a stern policeman stood in a corner. "Take your hood off, son," he said. Peter did so.

"Hi, Peter. I wonder if I can ask you a few questions." I tried to ease the sternness and sound non-threatening.

"I've got nothing to hide. I'm here voluntarily."

"What are you studying in college?" I leaned back in my chair.

He had been braced for other, harder questions, but seemed to relax at something familiar. "I'm working toward a bachelor's degree in social work with a minor in business."

Charlotte gave me a bright grin. "Perfect."

"Can I ask what this is all about?" He finally looked

up at us; the clear hazel eyes lined with doubt. "Are you some of the people I took things from? If so, I'm sorry. I just saw folks who needed them more."

Charlotte leaned forward. "Chief Poe tells me that you will probably get off with community service. Ms. Turner here has some ideas of what that might be if you are willing to listen to her."

He shrugged his shoulders. "Sure."

"Peter, I appreciate what you have been trying to do on your own. I wonder if you might be interested in doing that, only in a legal fashion."

That got his attention. "What do you mean?" His words were still edged in mistrust.

"I'd like to establish a non-profit foundation, start small, provide the items you've been, let's say, borrowing for people in need. We could look for a building to rent in that neighborhood. We would start out small, as I said, maybe work on getting donations, grants, that sort of thing. With your studies heading in that direction, might you be interested?"

"Would I ever!" He slapped his hand down on the table.

"Ms. Webb, Chief Poe, and I would like to arrange a meeting with the dean of the college. See what she thinks about the situation. You would need to keep your grades up; they couldn't slide. Since you are of age, we don't need your mother's permission, but we do want her support. Do you know where she is? I don't see her in your contact information."

"I think my mother would be happy to go along with it. She's been depressed since my dad died and living with a friend. She has been taking my mom to a therapy group. I've been ashamed to tell her about this. I just want her to be proud of me." He looked sad. "Helping all those people was kind of like I was helping her."

"Well, we'll take things as they go. First off, Chief Poe has agreed to attend your court appearance and suggest this alternative to the judge. He feels community service is a good option for you. If the judge agrees, we're all set."

Peter looked at Poe. "You would do that for me? After I broke the law?"

Poe nodded. "Special circumstances might be in order."

I continued. "If it all works out, it would be a slow process getting started. There's paperwork and legal issues, but Ms. Webb has agreed to help with that. I've arranged to set up a fund for start-up costs. We would then need to have a board of directors, possibly someone from the college might want to serve, maybe one or two of your professors or your advisor? Ms. Webb and I have talked about serving. Later, we might even find a way for students to volunteer, possibly for credit. Of course, this couldn't interfere with your schoolwork, and you would have to keep your grades up." I knew I was repeating myself, but I was just as eager as he seemed to be.

Peter sat stunned. It appeared this turn of events was the last thing he had imagined happening. "This all sounds like a dream. It's not some sort of entrapment, is it?" He was back to mistrust.

"Well, we have a lot of details to work out first, but I think this may be a better avenue for you to follow. As I said, it will be a slow process to get off the ground, but I think we can help a lot of people this way. I have so many ideas I would like to discuss with you, but let's meet after your sentencing. Would that work?"

Then he did the unimaginable. He stood up and raced around the table before Poe or the policeman could move and kissed me on the cheek.

Poe told me later I was blushing under my tears.

****

Email to El Turner

Dear Ms. Turner:

I hear I have you to thank for Paul the groom settling his bill. A thousand lucky stars on your house! If you send me the details of your birth, I will do your horoscope for free.

Yours in fate,
Madam Sasha

****

Email to Madam Sasha

Thanks for the email. I'm glad everything got straightened out.

Best,
El Turner
PS If I ever find out when my birthday is, I will take you up on your offer.

****

Email to El Turner

Well, that sounds mysterious! I never met anyone who didn't know their birth date. If you ever want to do a video chat, I would be glad to take some of your info and make an educated guess.

The fates await,
Madam Sasha

Chapter 16

"I can't believe you got all this together so quickly," Poe said a few weeks later.

The sentencing for Peter Barrie had gone as planned. With the approval of his dean, he and I had scouted a few buildings and had chosen one. It needed some work, but Peter assured me several other students had agreed to pitch in and help. I had spent several long days painting, rearranging, and overseeing the work that the landlord had agreed upon. He was thrilled with the improvements.

When I happened to meet Dolly Dee in the elevator one day and told her about the plans, she immediately convinced me to do a grand opening. She would even provide the entertainment, she said. A few days later she knocked at my door.

"I think I've got a good show planned. There's something for everyone."

"Your comedy, you mean?"

"Yes! And when I got word out, several other comedians agreed to give their time to such a worthy cause." Her enthusiasm was catching, but I tried to rein her in.

"You know this will be on a Saturday during the daylight hours. There will be children, so we can't have any 'adult only' content to the show. It will have to be squeaky clean."

She looked offended before grinning. "We can do

that! Chuckles might even be available."

"Chuckles?"

"Chuckles the Almost Clown. You must have heard of him."

"Cool. That would be great." I could only hope Chuckles wasn't a scary clown.

She must have seen my grimace. "Look, I know how organized you are. I will get you a play by play with who and what and when."

"Thank you, Dolly. That would be a big help. Things seem to be snowballing."

Charlotte worked hard getting all the city permits. She called with the good news. "Guess what. The mayor is even letting us block off a couple of streets. In exchange, he wants to say a few words."

"The mayor wants to come?"

"Something in this town that's getting attention? You can be sure he wants to be there! That's why a lot of the permits went through so quickly. Word travels fast. He is upset we did not invite him when the Parkville Historical Society was formed and now insists we have a grand opening later when the Hill House Museum is ready. That includes a grand speech by him." Charlotte sighed before continuing. "Then I got a call from the dean. She asked to speak as well. I guess we are going to need some kind of stage and microphone too. And if that's the case, you will need to grab the microphone. You started this."

"Oh, no. I will let whatever higher-ups want to praise what we are doing, just not me. And I guess we will need the stage and mike since we have several comedians performing."

"I hear the mayor wants to issue coins with your

picture on them."

I almost choked. "What? What! No."

"Only kidding, El. Take a breath."

"Thanks. This whole thing seems to have gotten so big. I imagined a small affair with a ribbon and scissors. I'll have to get Poe to give us a few policemen to manage the crowd."

"I believe the mayor is bringing his own big scissor." Charlotte laughed.

"Maybe it will rain." I was almost hoping for that.

"Now just keep smiling, and don't do any rain dances."

****

"You sure know how to throw a party," Poe commented later over dinner. I opened a bottle of wine, but I seemed to be the only one drinking it. Baths and wine had become my saviors these days. "On duty," he said when I offered him a glass. "Coffee?"

"Always on." I got up to pour him a cup.

"All the preliminaries seem to be taken care of, at least all the ones we have on the list. How is Peter doing?"

"We've been in almost constant communication. I think he is having a hard time concentrating on schoolwork. Good thing he's a wonderful student. He says several people have asked to perform along with Dolly and her troupe. One folk group and a poet who wrote a tribute just for the occasion. I think I will need an emcee so we don't run out of time."

"I bet Dolly would love to run the show. She seems to like to be in control. I think she could manage it," Poe said.

"You don't think she's too…" I searched for the

right word. "Boisterous?"

"She's full of life, and I think having someone upbeat and boisterous might do the trick. She's been on the road. She's used to crowds and noise. She's used to working in a time slot. If you give her a set of guidelines and limit time of the acts, I'm sure she'll do just fine. If the mayor and the dean want to speak, they should probably go first. Have the ribbon cutting, then the entertainment. That way the mayor will have his glory when the crowd is still fresh, and you can give them a printed time slot."

"Good idea. Thanks for all the help you are giving us." I shook my head. "What have I started here? If I want to do something like this again, please give me a rap on the noggin, okay?"

"I'm just glad it's working out." He looked over where Pan was sleeping under Albie's cage. "What's that all about?"

"They seem to be getting along. I've been leaving the office door open. Pan just wandered out one night and took up a space under Albie's cage. Albie kept peering over the edge of the cage, but he seems fine with it now. I think Albie has grown to like the doggy company. Luckily Peter has enough energy to come by almost every day and take Pan for a run. Tires them both out."

"You might have just changed that boy's life. El Turner. Saving birds and dogs and boys."

"Oh, please stop. I just get roped into things and, luckily, they have turned out for the best."

"I'll bring over your gold star tomorrow."

I finished off the wine. "I never knew how much work went into organizing something as simple as this community outreach. I didn't have to do much with the historical society when it was set up. Here the Board has drawn up a strict set of guidelines for starting out. They will probably reassess as we go along, but deciding who gets the help and what kind is important. Business skills are essential to make this work. They come up with issues I never would have imagined, but it all will be useful when we start applying for grants."

"What did you imagine?"

"That if a kid needed socks or a shirt, they could just walk in and get them."

"A simple goal in a complicated world." Poe poured another cup of coffee.

"You said it."

"Are you wishing for your old quiet life back?"

I had thought about that for almost a year now, and I had an answer for the moment. "No. I like what I have now."

Poe reached for my hand. "And who you have?"

"Absolutely."

****

"You weren't going to leave me out, were you?" The call was unexpected.

"Rita! How in the world did you hear about the grand opening?"

"Our dear Dolly filled me in."

"What? Since when do you and Dolly talk?"

"Remember she got my, ah, digits from you."

"Yes, I seem to remember that. Surely you aren't interested, are you?"

"I can smell a story from here."

"It's just a grand opening of a community resource. Nothing your big city folks are interested in reading."

"El, you know when I put my spin on something, everyone wants to read it."

"Well, this story has no dungeon or stolen money, I'm afraid."

"I am a bit sad you didn't tell me though."

"I'm sorry. I should have. After all, you are part sponsor of the whole event. You put in your part of the diamond reward money."

"145 664 823 144!" Albie shrieked.

"What in the world was that?" Rita asked over the phone.

"I said the D word."

"That is a clever bird. Give me all the details of this major happening in Parkville. I need to start gathering notes."

"Dolly is performing, but I'm sure she told you that."

"Yes, she wanted to know if I knew any New York comedians who might be interested in sharing the stage with her."

"She didn't."

"Oh yes, she did. My boss is looking into it. Feels it might juice up the story. New York sending comedic aid to Parkville. So, what else is happening?"

I told her about the mayor and the dean and all the speeches and Chuckles the Almost Clown.

"What about the boy? I want his whole life story."

"Peter?"

"Do you think he would give me an interview?"

"Don't see why not."

"I talked my editor into stretching this into a five-part series—Murder to Mercy. How do you like it?"

"Wow. You haven't lost your touch. You can tie it

all together?"

"Of course. When I'm done, it will be a ten-parter."

"No dungeons this time?"

"I'll let you know when my flight lands." I heard the smile over the phone.

****

"Now I know we have an occasion if Rita flies in," Poe told me later. "She wants to sit down with me while she's here. I told her the jewel case is mostly off limits for a bit. At least that was taken out of our hands. Seems Uncle Mickey's brother was wanted in a lot of places for a wide variety of things. Anyway, Rita's got a long list of people she wants to interview."

"I think she wants a human-interest story about Peter. You know, rags to philanthropist kind of thing. She should be in her glory."

"You look tired," Poe said. "Want me to take Pan for a walk?"

"Why don't we both go?"

"Why not indeed? You have the bags?"

"In every pocket I own."

****

"I can't believe this many people turned out," Ida shouted in my ear. "I think the whole town is here. I really can't believe that's my cousin up there performing comedy. And she is doing a great job as emcee. Did you see her buddy up to the mayor?"

"As long as he is in the picture, he loves it. Dolly's really good," I yelled back. "I didn't know what to expect, but I think she's exactly what this grand opening needed."

Ida tugged my arm and pulled me over to a quieter spot. "My aunt is going to get an earful from me. All those years she tried to steer Dolly into a singing career when she could have been doing what she clearly loved. All the time Dolly spent on the road is paying off. She sure knows how to work with the crowd.

"Better late than never."

"What I had to listen to over the years from her mother about those lowly bars and comedy clubs. Dives she called them. That practice really sharpened her skills and timing." Ida clapped her hands as Dolly finished her act and waved to hardy applause. "I'll say it again—I can't believe she's my cousin. I'm going to try and catch her and tell her." Ida moved away into the sea of humans.

I felt someone touch my arm and turned to see Poe there. "It's going well. You should be proud."

"I'm happy. Proud may come later when this is over."

"That's the quickest I've seen the mayor get off the stage. Wonder what happened."

"I think Rita asked him for an interview."

Poe laughed. "That will do it."

"Sshh. Peter's about to say a few words." I noticed he had exchanged his green hoodie for a crisp white button-down shirt and jeans. He looked sharp.

Peter had practiced his speech for me, so I knew what he was about to say, but I cried just the same. Looking around, I saw I wasn't the only one. There was a collective hush when he stopped, then a massive burst of clapping and shouting. Peter looked as embarrassed as one person could. He bowed and left the stage.

"Whee, girlie, you've done it again. What did this town do before you came here?"

"Sarge." I wiped away my tears. "You always say the sweetest things."

"Alan Poe. I've heard a lot about you." Poe extended his hand toward Will.

"Will Pepper. I could say the same thing where you're concerned."

Poe laughed. "Can I call you Sarge?"

"I'd be flap-jacked if you didn't."

I saw Peter heading my way. "If my two favorite gentlemen will excuse me for a minute, I want to have a few words with the man of the hour."

"Yes, Sarge and I will compare notes." Poe laughed.

"Be nice. And don't mention my name." I wagged my finger at both of them.

I threaded my way through the throng of admirers. "Peter! Congratulations! You did so well up there." I gave him a hug.

"Am I dreaming?" Peter had a dazed look on his face.

"Absolutely not. It's all real."

He looked like he wanted to say something more but was having a hard time getting it out. "I want to tell you. I mean, I want to say so much, but the words are stuck in my throat."

"Plenty of time for that. Just enjoy the day. Let's meet tomorrow and start going over some of the details."

"I'll be here. A few folks are giving up their Sunday to help stock shelves and tidy up. Then someone from the business department at school is going to shadow us for the first month or two just to make sure all the Board's guidelines are followed and our books are kept up. It will be more of a request and response trial run rather than an open store. That way someone won't have to be here all the time, like a manager. We can control the requests and try to fill them. For the present, we are only handling need-based inquiries from this area. We already have people asking for diapers, socks, shoes, and crutches. We also want to be able to deliver items to people who can't get out. Hopefully, we can expand that later."

"Have you thought of what you will name this business of yours?"

"I've been playing with the Rescue. What do you think?"

"Perfect." I noticed a line of people, mostly young girls, behind Peter. "I think there are a few folks who want to talk to you." I gestured behind him.

"Oh, I promised to put on a show for the kids. I brought Gertie."

"Gertie?"

"My friend Gertie." He pulled a colorful puppet out of his backpack and placed it on his hand.

"A sock puppet."

"Shhh. She doesn't know that. She can be a little crabby that way. She thinks she's real."

"Well, Gertie," I said to the puppet. "I think you are beautiful. Your hair is all the colors of the rainbow!"

"Gertie's beautiful," the puppet said and gave a mischievous cackle. "Gertie's a star."

"I know the kids will love Gertie."

Peter turned serious. "I really can't thank you enough. Who knows where I would be without your help." He looked ready to cry, so I lightly punched his arm.

"See you tomorrow, hero! Nice to meet you, Gertie!"

****

Email to El Turner

Dear Ms. Turner:

I have a strange request, and I'm not sure you can help or not.

Back story—My Great Aunt Hilly (Hildegard) is my mother's aunt. My Uncle Buster is my mother's brother. Uncle Buster used to live in Florida, but now he has moved to the city where we live. He drinks too much, is loud and annoying, and no one likes him, not even my mom. We never invite him to family holidays, but he always shows up. The problem is that he insults the memory of Great Aunt Hilly and calls her a hooker. He says he has proof she was a hooker. He calls her Hilly the Hooker. Since my name is Hillary, it sounds like he is referring to me. One Christmas I brought a boyfriend home, and Buster began his rant. My boyfriend thought he was talking about me, telling him family secrets. Although I explained, he stopped seeing me. My father usually takes Uncle Buster home when he gets like this and tells him he cannot come to family gatherings if he continues to be rude. Buster always promises, but never does. I wonder if there is some way you can prove Great Aunt Hilly was not a hooker.

Does that sound impossible?
Thank you.
Hillary Cunningham

****

Email to Hillary Cunningham
Hi Hillary—

Thank you so much for your email. I can understand how embarrassing this must be for you, especially with a similar name to your great aunt. Have you seen the proof your uncle has? If he has seen a census, certain terms like hooker were listed under occupation, but often those women were rug hookers in a rug factory. This might have been the case for your great aunt. Do you know what she did for a living? There were some tobacco-growing states that listed stripper as an occupation for people who stripped tobacco. You might ask for the proof or see if your mother has more information about what Hildegard did for a living.

If you would like to dig deeper, I can try a general search for her. I would need some of the information on the form attached. My fees are also listed there.

Good luck!
El Turner

****

"I guess I need an appointment to see you these days," Poe said. He had fed Albie and walked Pan while I finished up with emails.

"It's only for a short while," I answered while trying to type at the same time.

"Should I unpack the takeout or wait until you finish?"

"Unpack, please. I'm starving." I got up and closed the door to the office.

"I think the Rescue is up and running for now. Would you believe that someone taped the comedians at the grand opening, put it on social media sites, and we got a bunch of donations. We might be able to hire a manager to take charge so Peter can focus on his studies."

"Did you catch any of his puppet show for the kids? It was great!" Poe said.

"No, but I did get to meet Gertie."

Poe grinned. "What a character! She had everyone laughing. It almost seemed like she was real."

"Peter said he's already had requests for Gertie to give an encore performance at story hour at the library."

"If Rita gets wind of her success, she might want to do another interview. Look at this." Poe placed a New York newspaper on the table.

"Wow!" I grabbed the issue.

"Senor Marquez can't keep them in stock at his store, but he saved a copy I was to give to you."

"Part One. I'm sure that will stir some interest as well. From Murder to Mercy—she actually went with that title."

"Not enough drama for you?" Poe asked.

"Plenty. I just hope she didn't go overboard."

"She emailed me part of it to read, and it seemed fine. You're just happy if your name doesn't show up," Poe said.

"You were the one who said yes to an interview," I said. "Anyway, she concentrated on Finn's story and Peter's and how the two are connected."

"El, are you home?" I heard Jenny's voice at the door.

"Hi, Jenny. Come in. It feels like I haven't seen you in years!"

"I agree. Oh, hello, Inspector Poe. I hope I'm not disturbing anything."

"No. We were just talking about the grand opening and Rita's article."

"I won't bother you, but I wanted to give you an overdue thank you for the lovely teapot set. It's beautiful and such a thoughtful gift."

"Thank you, Jenny. It's a small token for all the care and help you've given me. I can't even begin to repay you."

"Do you have a minute? You can come down and see the gift, maybe have some tea?"

"That's a good idea, Jenny," Poe said. "I have to get back to work anyway."

"Thank you, Jenny. I'd be honored." I double locked the door as we left.

"Glad you have gotten into the habit," Poe said. "It only took a few break-ins and an attack."

"Hush!" We walked down the hallway to Jenny's door. "Look." I pointed out. "Jenny gets to keep her door open. What a luxury that must be."

I stepped into the room. "Surprise!" People appeared from other rooms, behind the furniture and curtains.

"What's going on?" I didn't think I was up for more excitement.

"It's a thank-you party for you," Jenny said, giving me a hug.

Poe's face was a broad smile. I saw Charlotte, Peter, Sarge, Ida, Dolly, Senor Marquez, Cassie, and a string of people from the Historical Society. I even got to meet the mysterious Mr. Sweetie, whose real name happened to be Mr. Sweeney. I told Poe he needed a hearing aid. A table loaded with sandwiches and cake stood in a corner. Streamers and balloons floated everywhere.

"I'm at a loss for words," I said. "You are the ones who should be thanked. You did all the work."

Jenny put her arm through mine. "Rita was sorry she couldn't be here, but she sent a special guest in her place."

I looked around in confusion.

"It's me! I'm the special guest!" Gertie cried as she appeared from behind the sofa, her rainbow locks flipping back and forth. "Cake!" she cried. "Me first. The biggest piece, please, for Gertie! Then El."

I went from person to person, sharing a hug, thanking them again for their kindness.

"Speech," someone shouted.

I looked around at the friends I had made since coming to Parkville. All the tragedy and comedy that had developed. All the emotion. I felt my throat well up and couldn't stop the waterfall of tears.

"I'll leave that to Gertie," I sniffed.

****

"Well, another non-profit success in the books. Another fun-loving creature in the books. Another murder in the books," Poe said.

"Please, no more. That's one too many for my books." We were sitting in my living room. Poe had helped me pick out a new easy chair that was delivered that day. One that was more me, one that suited us better, and one that brightened up the room. Now that my office had been moved to the second bedroom and the table was clear of clutter, it seemed like more of a home. A new kitchen table was next. Albie fit right in. So did Pan. No one had claimed him. I accepted fate and bought a better collar and leash, new bowls, and better food. I took him to the vet and again to the groomer.

"So, you have one puzzle solved. At least you know where you came from." Poe hadn't brought up my talk with Finn during the upheaval that had been my life. He was waiting until I was ready. Now seemed like the right time.

"I'm still not sure who I am."

"But didn't Anne Marie fill you in?"

"Who?"

"Anne Marie Finnegan. Your mother's partner."

"Oh. She just told me to call her Finn." I sat back and gave him the short version of my meeting with her. I tried not to hit the low points.

"She said you were picked up in New Mexico?"

"I've been thinking about that. Maybe my family were vacationing and stopped at that rest area? Like we had to use the facilities or to let the kids play and I had wandered away. Finn said they had the van open, and I crawled in and fell asleep. They didn't notice it until later."

"Well, that is certainly strange!" Poe almost choked on his drink.

"How so?"

"You don't see the similarities?" He stared at me in disbelief.

"What are you talking about?"

"The same day you find out that you quietly slipped into someone's van, a dog just happens to quietly slip into your car."

I couldn't catch my breath. "What? You can't be serious? What?"

"Odd coincidence."

"My mother always said life held no coincidences; we just didn't see the connection yet."

"Well, that one will take a lot of thinking. What will you do now? Is it satisfying get on with life?"

"Of course it is. I don't feel like this one is over though. I still don't know who I am, and I found out my birthday is not my birthday. I don't know how old I am. Then there is the strange similarity of me and the dog. Not to mention the canned soup. I feel like my life is being shaped from some sort of shadow world."

"Canned soup?"

"Oh, I was boring Rita with my life story, and I mentioned one place I had stayed was with an older lady who had a pantry full of canned soup. That's all we ate."

"Okay, now you are freaking me out. No more coincidence or connections please."

"So, Mr. Freak Out, do I keep searching to find the real me or do I accept who I am and go from there? The world has shifted so far one way, and I feel like I'm climbing a big hill."

"Please don't turn into Sisyphus."

"Don't go throwing Greek myths my way. Not today anyway."

"Why? What else happened?"

After all the highs, I was also dealing with my share of lows. "I didn't want to say anything, but I'm getting kicked out."

"You can't be serious! On what grounds?"

"The apartment is not renewing my lease here. Too many broken doors and too much commotion for the other members of the building. A big barking dog and a bird who cries *Murder* at every turn. Guess I'll have to check out the other apartments in the area. See which ones are pet friendly. I hate to move away from Jenny. All my memories of Rita took place here. When I think about it, I turn into a puddle."

"Well, don't go wallowing around just yet." Poe took my hand in his. "Maybe I can come up with a solution."

"You? What?"

"I have a big old house that sits empty most of the day. I think we could find a quiet spot for you to set up a computer. The whole second floor is unused. It's mostly bedrooms, but you could have your choice. I have a studio above the garage if that would work better. It hasn't been used in a while, but there are sunny windows for Albie and a fenced backyard for Pan. You can come by any time and see if there's a place that would suit you and your entourage."

"Why, Chief Poe! Aren't you afraid people will talk?"

"They talk anyway, so what's the difference? I could charge you rent if that would make you feel less like a kept woman."

"Can I check it out first? I don't want to be a burden. And what if we ever…" I didn't finish the sentence.

He just shrugged and tried diversion. "We'll take each day as it comes. By the way, did you ever get results from that DNA kit?"

"Yes. I'm also in their database. I gave them my email address and phone."

"I have been wanting to talk this over with you for a while, but it never seemed like the right moment. After you've moved—wherever you move to—I think it's time for that trip to Hawaii. I think it's been in the plans, and we can both use some distance from Parkville for a bit."

I sat up. "I'm certain it is, Chief of Police Poe. Does this mean you can get some time off?"

"Yes. They owe it to me."

"Let me look at my calendar to see what I need to finish. Most of my research is at a standstill." I went to the computer. "See, empty spots on the calendar. I don't think I have any new projects. Let me get my phone."

I turned my phone on. One voicemail. "Well, just shows I haven't checked my phone in quite some time." I listened in shock and then called Poe into the office.

He ambled over.

I pressed play again. "Hello, El Turner. I was notified we might be a DNA match and wonder if we could talk. My name is Jacqueline Collins, and I think I'm your aunt."

A word about the author…

Allison Thorpe published six collections of poetry before turning her love of writing to cozy mysteries. She and her husband spent several decades enjoying a homesteader lifestyle in rural Kentucky where they built their own home and tended an organic garden. She taught college courses in English Literature, Creative Writing, and Women's Studies before moving to Lexington, Kentucky, where she works as a writing mentor at The Carnegie Center for Literacy and Learning. https://allisonthorpe.weebly.com/

Thank you for purchasing
this publication of The Wild Rose Press, Inc.

For questions or more information
contact us at
info@thewildrosepress.com.

The Wild Rose Press, Inc.
www.thewildrosepress.com

Milton Keynes UK
Ingram Content Group UK Ltd.
UKHW021917281024
450365UK00017B/827